THE CHAMELEON OF KRAKOW

Gordon Wallis

Copyright © [2024] by [Gordon Wallis]

All rights reserved.

No portion of this book may be reproduced in any form without written permission from the publisher or author, except as permitted by U.S. copyright law.

Contents

Prologue. Undisclosed coastal compound, Nugal region, Puntland, Somalia. 1

1. Chapter One. London. Present day. 4
2. Chapter Two. One month previously. 11.05 pm. Undisclosed coastal compound, Nugal region, Puntland, Somalia. 8
3. Chapter Three. 16
4. Chapter Four. 18
5. Chapter Five. 20
6. Chapter Six. 22
7. Chapter Seven. 24
8. Chapter Eight. 30
9. Chapter Nine. 34
10. Chapter Ten. 41
11. Chapter Eleven. 43
12. Chapter Twelve. 45
13. Chapter Thirteen. 48
14. Chapter Fourteen. 50
15. Chapter Fifteen. 53
16. Chapter Sixteen. 58
17. Chapter Seventeen. 60

18. Chapter Eighteen. 62
19. Chapter Nineteen. 64
20. Chapter Twenty. 66
21. Chapter Twenty-One. 71
22. Chapter Twenty-Two. 73
23. Chapter Twenty-Three. 78
24. Chapter Twenty-Four. 80
25. Chapter Twenty-Five. 82
26. Chapter Twenty-Six. 88
27. Chapter Twenty-Seven. 91
28. Chapter Twenty-Eight. 93
29. Chapter Twenty-Nine. 95
30. Chapter Thirty. 97
31. Chapter Thirty-One. 99
32. Chapter Thirty-Two. 101
33. Chapter Thirty-Three. 103
34. Chapter Thirty-Four. 105
35. Chapter Thirty-Five. 107
36. Chapter Thirty-Six. 110
37. Chapter Thirty-Seven. 112
38. Chapter Thirty-Eight. 114
39. Chapter Thirty-Nine. 116
40. Chapter Forty. 118
41. Chapter Forty-One. 120
42. Chapter Forty-Two. 124
43. Chapter Forty-Three. 127

44.	Chapter Forty-Four.	129
45.	Chapter Forty-Five.	131
46.	Chapter Forty-Six.	133
47.	Chapter Forty-Seven.	136
48.	Chapter Forty-Eight.	138
49.	Chapter Forty-Nine.	140
50.	Chapter Fifty.	142
51.	Chapter Fifty-One.	145
52.	Chapter Fifty-Two.	149
53.	Chapter Fifty-Three.	151
54.	Chapter Fifty-Four.	158
55.	Chapter Fifty-Five.	160
56.	Chapter Fifty-Six, Krakow, Poland, Two Weeks Later.	183
	Dear Reader	190

Prologue. Undisclosed coastal compound, Nugal region, Puntland, Somalia.

The fierce afternoon sun scorched the landscape, its relentless rays turning the sandy expanse into a blinding sea of light. Tiny fragments of mica scattered across the ground gleamed menacingly, hurling sharp glints of sunlight directly into Darius's eyes. Unaccustomed to such brilliance, he squinted painfully, his vision blurred by the harsh illumination. The air was thick with heat and humidity, an oppressive blanket that smothered every breath and made his filthy skin sticky with sweat. The sudden transition from the dim, stifling confines of the cell to the chaotic, overwhelming open air was jarring. Confusion swirled in Darius's mind, a tumultuous storm that mirrored the swirling sands around his feet.

Everything about that afternoon felt perilously wrong, as if the very air buzzed with the threat of impending disaster. The men who had gathered to watch bore a febrile air of excitement; their eyes gleaming with an intensity that bordered on ferocity. It was as though they were spectators at some ancient gladiatorial contest, their anticipation for the unfolding spectacle tinged with a deep, unsettling aggression. Perhaps it was bloodlust that animated their dark features and lent a palpable tension to the atmosphere; whatever it was, it was clear that the situation boded ill for Darius and Trevor.

Amidst the cacophony of foreign voices and the oppressive heat, an overwhelming sense of dread settled heavily upon Darius's shoulders. He could feel the eyes of the crowd upon him, their gazes sharp as knives, cutting through the confusion and fear that threatened to engulf him. The air seemed to thicken with each passing moment, the humidity wrapping around him like paralysing chains, dragging him deeper into the heart of this unsettling and dangerous spectacle.

"Pick up the pipe, Darius..." said Omar quietly, his brown eyes burning with a combination of rage and wild hysteria.

Darius Ayman stood panting and blinking in the blazing mid-afternoon sunlight and stared down at the heavy, 2-foot length of hollow steel that lay in the sand at his feet. His body now rake thin and his clothes in filthy tatters, he was a dried-out husk of his former self and by the expression on his face, it was clear he was a man whose spirit had been broken. Omar gritted his teeth in frustration and glanced briefly at Suleiman. The old man barked an order in his guttural, native Somali and his thin face shook with anticipation. Omar then turned to face the trembling figure of Darius once again.

"I said, pick up the pipe," he hissed furiously. "Do it now or Sulieman will kill you. The choice is yours. It's you or him..."

Tears began to carve rivulets in the dirt on Darius Ayman's hollowed cheeks and trickled into his scruffy beard as he stared down at the curled-up figure of his colleague. Barely conscious and severely emaciated, Trevor opened his sleep-encrusted eyes and blinked as he looked up at his friend standing above him.

"He is sick! Look at him!" shouted Omar, his patience rapidly disappearing "The man will be dead soon, anyway! Pick up the pipe! Now!!"

The other men who stood around to witness the occasion began to jeer and stomp about with rabid excitement and bloodlust as the tension built. Their gowns and headscarves blew gently in the salt-laden wind. Sulieman Abdi, their elderly leader, stood up from the cheap plastic chair placed in the sand nearby. He lifted the AK47 rifle and raised it as he stepped towards Darius. The thin skin of his cheek bulged with a chewed-up ball of khat, and he spat a gooey gob of brown saliva onto the sand as he approached. He spoke a brief command in his native Somali which Omar repeated in English.

"Pick up the pipe, Darius," he said quietly, his head tilted and his eyes wide "If you do not do as I say immediately, your own life will be over in a matter of seconds. This is my final warning..."

Darius Ayman stooped his rake-thin body and lifted the heavy pipe with his right hand. His breathing had become ragged his eyes were wide with primal terror and madness. The jeering and screaming from the other men became frenzied as he straightened his frame and stared down at the pathetic figure of the man who had been his friend and co-pilot for over 5 years. Despite his illness, 57-year-old Trevor Nichol lifted himself up from the sand on his right elbow and looked Darius in the eye. As he did so he shook his head from side to side and repeatedly mouthed the word,

'No...!'

But it was then that the older man, Suleiman Abdi stepped forward once again and held the ugly muzzle of the automatic rifle inches from Darius's head. Both Sulieman and Omar were screaming now, flecks of spittle flying from their purple lips, and the sound drowned out the raucous cacophony of the watchers. With wide, delirious eyes, Darius Ayman lifted the heavy pipe and held it high above his head, ready to make the killing blow. Finally accepting his inevitable fate, Trevor Nichol shook his head slowly, closed his eyes and lay down in the sand in a foetal position, his bony hands covering his ears in a final, futile effort to muffle the appalling death racket that surrounded him.

"Kill him!" screamed Omar while Sulieman and the others screamed the same in Somali.

"KILL HIM!!"

1

Chapter One. London. Present day.

"You're talking about pirates," I said, "Somali pirates?"

"They're all cut from the same filthy cloth," growled Colonel Callum Jackson. "Fucking savages the lot of them. I wouldn't be surprised if they are former pirates. However, there have been no major incidents reported in Somali waters for the past five years. The International Chamber of Shipping has declared that the region is no longer designated a high-risk area. But we're talking about a failed state that has had no real government for the past thirty years. The place is a fucking hellhole. And now these numbskulls have worked out a new way of fleecing cash from the civilised world. Kidnapping foreigners and aid workers. Biting the very hand that feeds them!"

I had received the call at 9.00 am sharp. It had come as a surprise, given that my last encounter with Colonel Callum Jackson had resulted in me giving him a fractured jaw. I had been making coffee in my London flat when the call came through and I immediately recognised the voice. His South African secretary and I had spoken before and once again I had been summoned for a meeting at his suite in the swanky Savoy Hotel. A multi-millionaire ex-soldier, he had formed the notorious Jackson Advisory Group after his time in the army in various countries in southern Africa. Although currently involved in the business of de-mining and high-level security, it was common knowledge that the organization was a mercenary outfit that had been involved in both propping up and removing several nasty dictators in and around Africa. We had butted heads on several occasions and this latest call to see him had come completely unexpectedly. The colonel sighed deeply and reached for the crystal decanter that stood on the left-hand side of his expansive, antique desk.

"Whisky?" he grumbled as he removed the chunky stopper.

I glanced at my watch to see it had just gone 12.15 pm. *A bit early, Green.*

"Why not," I replied.

I watched closely as the tough old soldier poured two stiff tots into squat crystal tumblers. *Miserable bastard.* He pushed one glass towards me which I lifted and brought to my nose to smell.

"Macallan, triple cask matured, 15 years old," he grunted as he took a gulp of the golden nectar "Not bad..."

I winced as the powerful spirit went down leaving a pleasant, woody taste in my mouth.

"Not bad at all," I replied.

The big man stood up from his desk and I could see that, despite his advancing age, he was still physically fit and strong. *Not someone to be messed with.* He turned around and pulled a black cotton sheet away from a whiteboard that had been set up behind his desk.

The board showed a map of North Africa centred on Somalia. The various regions of that country were marked clearly. Jackson raised his left hand and pointed at the coastal area.

"This is Puntland," he said, rocking softly on the balls of his feet. "From what we know, an absolute shithole. A vast wasteland of scrub and sand that reaches from the coast far into the interior of the country. Access is poor and roads are rough, so any interaction with the cockroaches who dwell there has been mostly done by air or sea in the past. It's remote, isolated and lawless. And I'm sure I don't have to tell you, Green, extremely dangerous."

The big man sighed and turned to sit down at his desk once again. As he did so, he adjusted the paisley cravat around his thick, suntanned neck. I placed the heavy tumbler on the desk in front of me and readied myself to speak. I could see that the man was in no mood for pleasantries, so I decided to get straight to business.

"So," I said, looking him in the eye, "why am I here, Colonel?"

I had read the mood correctly and he cleared his throat before speaking.

"Three months ago, a pair of pilots made an unexpected stop in Mogadishu in Somalia. They work for a sizable Polish transport company headquartered in Krakow. Typically, these pilots never disembark in Mogadishu. Too dangerous. They simply load their cargo and continue to their next destination. However, this time, they encountered a problem and were delayed. Consequently, these two pilots had to secure a room in a nearby hotel and that very night they were both kidnapped. Their captors eventually initiated contact with their superiors in Poland about a week later. Since then, prolonged negotiations have been ongoing between the Polish company and the kidnappers. To handle these negotiations, the company hired a negotiator—an ex-British Army professional with specialized skills. Now, the Polish company and the negotiator believe they are close to reaching an agreement and finalizing the ransom amount for the release of the two pilots. This is where we come in. The Jackson Advisory Group has been contacted, and we've been tasked with delivering the ransom."

I listened calmly and inquired, "How is this typically done?"

The man leaned back in his chair, took a sip of whisky and replied,

"Well, in the past, when dealing with sea-based piracy, ransoms were often dropped from an aircraft into the sea near the captured vessel. The pirates would then retrieve the dropped package, check its contents and release the hijacked ship's crew to continue their journey. Sometimes these negotiations took up to a year to conclude. These people have no regard for time and during the wait, the health of the prisoners deteriorates, often leading to fatalities."

Colonel Jackson sighed deeply and took another glug of whisky.

"To cut a long story short, the company believes they are close to an agreement and need someone with knowledge of Africa, someone trustworthy and capable, to deliver a substantial amount of money and secure the release of the prisoners."

I nodded, understanding the background.

"So, given the change in circumstances, how can a ransom be safely delivered now that the kidnappers are on land? How do you ensure the prisoners' release?"

He sipped again and leaned forward.

"This is another problem, the leader of this band of merry men is outright refusing to have a ransom delivered by helicopter. By all accounts, he's a paranoid son of a bitch and although it makes total sense to deliver it by helicopter and simply pick up the prisoners and fly them out, he will have none of it. It has been flatly refused. The safest method we've devised is by sea. Once an agreement is reached, the money will be transported to a company vessel which is already stationed off the coast of Somalia. The designated person will access the coast using a small, high-speed boat. Upon arrival, there will be a meeting and exchange—the money for the prisoners. Once all parties are satisfied, the prisoners will be handed over and will leave on the same boat to the mother ship where the waiting helicopter will whisk them away. Attempting to deliver the ransom by road is out of the question. These are their demands. It will only be done by boat."

"So, you want me to be in charge of delivering this ransom?"

The big man nodded,

"Yes, Green. If you decide to take the job, the compensation will be substantial. The Polish company, Kaminsky Logistica, are anxious to secure the release of their pilots. They are close to making a deal with these scumbags and they need to get ready now. My secretary has a file with all the details; pick it up on your way out and review it. I expect your decision by 4:00 pm. this afternoon. Now, I have other business to attend to. It's been a pleasure seeing you again, Green. Goodbye."

I held his gaze for a moment, contemplating my disdain for the man. Then, I swallowed the last of my whisky, placed the heavy tumbler on the desk and spoke.

"Thank you, Colonel. I'll get back to you."

As I left the office, the efficient Afrikaner secretary handed me a thin red file. I thanked her and left the hotel suite. As I headed towards the elevators, I couldn't help but curse the trouble this man had brought into my life. However, I knew I couldn't ignore it. The remuneration, if I accepted, would undoubtedly be highly enticing. *No such thing as easy money, Green!*

On the ground floor, I walked out of the elevator and made my way across the chequered marble floor to the hotel's revolving doors. The limousine driver, who had brought me from my flat in North London, stood nearby bundled up against the cold. I stepped into the Rolls Royce, sank into the cigar and cologne-scented leather interior and opened the file. The chauffeur slid smoothly into the driving seat and glanced at me in the rearview mirror before speaking.

"Heading back home, sir?"

"Yes, back home," I replied looking up from the file.

2

Chapter Two. One month previously. 11.05 pm. Undisclosed coastal compound, Nugal region, Puntland, Somalia.

British-born 57-year-old pilot Captain Trevor Nichol opened his eyes and forced himself to sit up with his back against the rough concrete wall. He lifted his emaciated arms and rubbed the sleep from his eyes wincing from the dull pain in his stomach. The peptic ulcer, which was the cause of this discomfort, had largely been cured by a combination of medication and the careful diet he had been keeping since his diagnosis over a year ago. Initially, it had been treated with simple antibiotics, histamines and antacids so that soon after, the symptoms had miraculously disappeared. But this alone was not enough to satisfy his beloved wife who had prepared a strict diet for him going forward. This consisted of bottled water, probiotics and high-fibre foods along with plenty of fresh fruit and vegetables. Although, given the nature of his job as a cargo pilot plying routes in the north of Africa, it had been sometimes difficult to stick to. He had always managed to smuggle enough bran flakes, supplements and vitamins along with him on his 6-week contracts. Of course, there had always been the possibility of collecting fresh fruit from the various pickup and drop-off points he found himself in. Grapes and mangoes could be found year-round in Egypt while there were plentiful watermelons, dates and oranges to be had in Libya. His fitness had improved, the ulcer had healed nicely and had been largely forgotten until that fateful night 3 months ago. The night when everything changed.

Mogadishu, Somalia, although a regular destination, was not a city they would usually stop in for any length of time. Normally, the ground time would be no longer than an hour or two and then they would take off. But on that day, there had been a delay with their cargo pickup and he and his co-pilot had been forced to take a room at a hotel near the airport. 43-year-old Egyptian-born Darius Ayman and he had been pleasantly surprised by the cleanliness and pleasant atmosphere of the establishment and had eaten a fine dinner followed by the sinking of a few beers on the balcony overlooking the airport. The cargo was due to be loaded during the night and the plan had been to head back to the airport early the following morning and continue with their flight east to Addis Ababa in Ethiopia. Their working contracts saw them spending 6 weeks at a time plying the routes of North Africa before returning to their wives and families for 2 months of downtime. Although nowhere near as glamorous as flying for one of the world's major airlines, the job was well paid and the two months off with their families was, for the two men, priceless. The Polish-based company, Kaminski Logistika, was family-owned and took great care of its staff at all levels. A global player in the heavy goods transport business, it boasted a fleet of cargo ships and 40,000 road haulage trucks operating in Europe along with the aviation division of the company which employed both Trevor and Darius. But it had been that very night in the airport hotel in Mogadishu, the capital of the war-torn country of Somalia, that it all went wrong.

The two pilots had retired to their adjoining rooms early at around 9.30 pm and both men had been fast asleep when it happened. Their attackers had somehow obtained duplicate keys for their rooms and had entered silently under cover of darkness. Both had weapons held to their heads and had been bound and gagged to prevent any resistance. With military precision, they had been frog-marched, blindfolded, down the fire escape stairway and bundled into a waiting vehicle.

The subsequent journey had taken over 24 hours travelling over rough roads north into Puntland passing the regional capital of Garowe before turning right and heading through the wastelands down to the coast. During this harrowing journey, both Trevor and Darius had been made to cower in the footwell at the rear of the vehicle and been kicked and prodded with gun barrels any time they protested. Their captors had seemingly no English and loud music had been blaring the whole way. It had been in the dead of night when finally, they had been pulled from the vehicle, stiff, dehydrated and confused then thrown into the filthy concrete walled room that had been their prison for the past three months.

At the time, the only clue the two captive men had of their location was the fact that the air was salty and the view from the tiny window was that of a desolate prospect of sand and plastic rubbish. The bars in the window of their cell were rusted and, during the day, seagulls could be seen and heard squawking above. At roughly 7 by 4 metres in size, their prison was dark and squalid with no running water and only a crude brick hole in the right-hand corner to use as a toilet. The heavy corrugated steel roof was bolted and welded to thick bars embedded in the concrete of the walls. There were no mattresses, no blankets and no seats, nothing remotely resembling any furniture or human comforts at all. Trevor and Darius had spent the first days desperately trying to talk to their captors to find out what exactly was going on. But deep down, both men knew exactly the situation in which they had found themselves. They had become part of an ever-growing statistic of Westerners who had been kidnapped in Somalia.

For one week, Trevor and Darius had been largely ignored and only fed scraps of flatbread and a watery gruel of goat meat gravy in a battered aluminium pot. Despite their constant pleas, the man who delivered these meagre rations spoke no English and showed no interest in conversing with them. Dressed in dirty robes with a silken blue scarf wrapped around his head, the only part of his face that was visible was his eyes. Darius had tried on many occasions to converse with the man in his native Arabic, but this had been to no avail. The man simply delivered the daily pittance of food and left. It was clear, however, that their holding cell was near a settlement. Loud, distorted music would play from sunrise every day and continue without stopping until long after sunset. Manic laughter could also be heard nearby and quite often there would be random gunfire and drunken cheering. Trevor Nichol and Darius Ayman had spent a full 5 days holed up in this airless, stinking hellhole with daytime temperatures reaching the high 40s and the nights spent in teeth-chattering cold as the mists from the nearby ocean rolled in.

But it was on the 6th morning that the thick steel door had been swung open and the prisoners were called out at gunpoint. Half starved, filthy dirty and confused, they had been struck with gun butts and kicked into position, sitting in the dust with their backs to the bricks of their cell. Blinking through the sudden bright sunlight, they had finally laid eyes on their captors. A seemingly ragtag group of 10 Somali men, they wore the sweeping robes that most men of their age wore in the region. All had the thin faces, aquiline noses, dark skin and high foreheads of native Somalians. Some of the men wore headscarves while others were bare headed revealing their characteristic straight hair. All the men were armed with AK47 assault rifles and most seemed agitated and nervous with many of them showing cheeks bulging with balls of chewed-up khat.

The buds and leaves of the khat plant are chewed for stimulant and euphoric effect with long-term use associated with mental health conditions like amphetamine psychosis.

It has also been associated with depression, mood swings and violent behaviour which was something both Trevor Nichol and Darius Ayman were to learn very soon. It was then that the leader of the men stepped forward and took a seat on a cheap plastic chair. Older than the rest of the men, his face was fleshless and the skin on his cheekbones was like brown parchment. The veins in his sunken temples throbbed and he had a nervous, twitchy demeanour. He stared at the two men with cold, bloodshot eyes and shouted in Arabic for another of the men to come and sit at his side. A second, younger man with a fuller, rounded face stepped forward and took a seat in the sand to the left of the leader. With another shouted command from the leader, the second man spoke.

"Good morning," he said in a slight American accent as he pulled a sheet of paper from under his robe "You men are pilots for the Polish company, Kaminski Logistika. Trevor Nichol and Darius Ayman. Is that correct?"

Captain Trevor Nichol cleared his throat and answered.

"That is correct," he said quietly "Who are you and what do you want from us?"

Suddenly there was an unholy outburst from the leader who spat out a huge gob of khat and screamed at the two men while pointing his weapon at their faces. The two pilots cowered in the dust at the sudden, unexpected outburst. It was a full minute later when the second man spoke once again.

"For your own safety," he said calmly in perfect English "Unless otherwise asked, you will answer my questions with a simple yes or no in future. Is that clear?"

Trevor Nichol glanced briefly at Darius who sat in wide-eyed terror next to him.

"Yes..." he replied.

"Good," said the second man "Then your lives will be a lot easier in future. My name is Omar, and I will be your translator. You are now prisoners of Mr Suleiman Abdi. He is the man sitting on the chair next to me. I am advising you not to look him in the eyes at any time. Trust me, it will be better if you take heed of my words. Your company has been informed that you are now our prisoners, and a telephone call has been arranged for 3.00 pm. this afternoon. The purpose of this audience is to inform you of the situation and what will take place later today. You will have an opportunity to send messages to your families and to talk to your principals this afternoon. If our negotiations are successful, you will be released soon and will be free to return to your families. Do you have any questions?"

"What is it you want?" asked Trevor quietly.

Omar smiled and then chuckled to himself as he relayed the question in the guttural-sounding Somali dialect to the rest of the men. Suddenly there was an outburst of frantic laughter and hooting and jeering as the men almost collapsed in mirth. Their wide gapped teeth were stained ochre from the chewed-up khat. It took a full minute for this to die down and for Omar to speak once again.

"Money," he said, still grinning. "Your company will have to pay a ransom if they want to see you again. It's as simple as that. Now, you will return to your accommodation and be ready for the phone call this afternoon. Is everything clear? Are there any more questions?"

There was an extended pause as Trevor glanced at Darius who sat there, still with a look of pure terror on his grimy face. Eventually, he turned back to Omar and spoke.

"We are starving, and we both need to bathe," he said, "Will this be possible?"

Omar turned his head and spoke quietly to the leader, Suleiman. The older man raised his eyes, spat another gob of discoloured saliva onto the sand in front of Trevor and spoke in a guttural mumble. Omar nodded and turned once again to Trevor.

"You are being given food and water," he said calmly "That is all for now. How long you are here will be determined by your company. Now, stand up slowly and make your way back into your cell. No sudden movements, please gentlemen."

The phone call had been made as promised and both prisoners had been brought out into the open to witness it. The interpreter, Omar, had been polite while introductions had been made and their captors had sat listening attentively throughout. Initially, proof of life had been requested by the company owner, Marek Kaminski and photographs had been taken and sent by WhatsApp. Afterwards, both Trevor and Darius had been allowed to speak to their boss for a minute each after which the phone was handed back to Omar. With initial contact established, an arrangement for a subsequent call was made for the same time the following day, the call had been cut off and the prisoners returned to their cell. This had marked the beginning of an agonizingly slow and protracted set of negotiations for their release.

THE CHAMELEON OF KRAKOW

Suleiman Abdi's initial demand had been for ten million United States dollars. Both Trevor Nichol and Darius Ayman had been shocked when their boss had calmly made a counteroffer of only $200.000.00. This had been immediately scoffed at by their captors and the line had been cut. During their long hours of dark captivity, both prisoners had discussed this seemingly paltry offer the company had made for their lives, but it had been concluded that this represented a starting point. Both men were aware that time was no issue for their captors, and they may well have to spend up to a year in captivity before an agreement was reached. But it was soon after that Trevor Nichol became unwell once again and his stomach ulcer began weakening him and causing serious discomfort. Day after day they had been fed the same gruel and the meagre supply of brackish water was never enough. Both men had begged for some relief, but their pleas had consistently fallen on deaf ears.

It had been two weeks into this ordeal when the young boy from the nearby compound had started visiting their cell in the dead of night. At maybe 12 years old, the boy would arrive at around 11.00 pm. Having taken pity on the two prisoners, the boy would bring a small plastic Tupperware box of rice and stew along with a 2-litre bottle of fresh water. It was these nightly visits from the boy that had kept Trevor and Darius alive during the long months of captivity. Determined to keep morale and positivity up, both men had started exercising during the cooler hours in the evenings. But Trevor Nichol's illness had returned in earnest and soon he was unable to do this as his body had begun wasting away despite the small rations of extra food.

Time and time again, Trevor and Darius had been allowed a minute to speak to their boss, Marek Kaminski, but he had always sounded cold and somewhat indifferent to their plight. This was both terrifying and puzzling to the two men and night after night, they ruminated on why this would be the case. Their company was well known for caring about the welfare of its employees and it appeared something was amiss. Their desperate pleas seemed to be falling on deaf ears and the failing health of Trevor Nichol was of no concern at all. All the while, their captor, Suleiman Abdi, was losing patience with the situation while negotiations continued. This while his prisoners starved. Still, the young boy would deliver the extra food and water each night and sit silently outside the window while they ate. Although he said very little, it was out of the kindness of his heart and a feeling of pity that he did this, and Darius and Trevor made sure he knew how grateful they were. If it had not been for him, they would surely have been dead by then.

During that harrowing period, Darius and Trevor found themselves haunted by the visits of an exceptionally vile and unwelcome figure, known to them solely by the name Faizal. This man had been born with a cleft palate and as a result, his face and lips were distorted and disfigured. He also harboured a perverse and unsettling fascination with the two prisoners, manifesting itself in actions that were both bizarre and malevolent. Often, without any discernible reason, he would appear at their cell window in the afternoons, not to offer solace or company, but to mock and deride them. Often, he would simply spit gobs of green khat-infused saliva through the bars of the cell at them. His presence was a dark cloud, filled with malice.

Faizal's cruelty knew no bounds. There were instances when he would bring scraps of food, only to conspicuously consume them before the starving eyes of Darius and Trevor, revelling in their despair. His face bore the marks of his twisted nature; with wide-set, gapped teeth and the twisted upper lip and distorted nose of his born condition, it seemed to mirror the ugliness within. But it was not just his appearance that instilled fear - it was his actions. With a sadistic glee, he would sometimes thrust his weapon through the cell's thick bars, mimicking gunshots with sickening enthusiasm, cocking the weapon menacingly as if to fire, terrorizing them further.

This man had become the embodiment of fear and loathing for the two prisoners. They were baffled and tormented by the sheer inexplicability of his cruelty, unable to fathom what drove him to delight so in their suffering. His visits were a constant reminder of their helpless plight, each encounter with him a psychological torment that left scars far deeper than the physical confines of their cell.

Despondency and a deep sense of depression had taken hold as the days dragged on in an endless cycle of threats and abuse. This combined with the incessant distorted music that would blare from the compound from dawn till dusk. Mindless and repetitive, it was a special form of torture. That combined with the cockroaches, the random gunfire and drunken cheering and shouting, created a maddening, appalling atmosphere which became a marathon of untold suffering. It was around that time that the prisoners had accepted that it was quite likely that they would perish in that barren, baking wasteland on the desolate coast of Puntland, Somalia.

Sitting upright now, Trevor Nichol watched as Darius stood at the tiny window holding on to the thick rusted steel bars.

THE CHAMELEON OF KRAKOW

As usual, a whispered conversation was made with the boy as he handed the prisoners the Tupperware box and the bottle of water. The food and water were shared and consumed quickly while the boy waited. It was once the plastic box and empty bottle were returned through the bars that the boy stood and whispered another message. Darius listened attentively and watched as the boy left, making his way back to the nearby compound across the sand in the moonlight. The news had been disturbing and Darius came to sit with Trevor in the darkness to discuss it immediately afterwards. Exhausted and in great discomfort, Trevor Nichol listened as Darius spoke.

"Suleiman is unhappy with the slow pace of negotiations with Kaminski," he said quietly "The men had a meeting earlier tonight and the boy was listening to their discussion."

"And what did they say?" said Trevor, panting slightly as he wiped the sweat from his forehead.

"Suleiman was accusing Marek of not being sincere. He said that if they don't get a firm offer soon, they will have to send a clear message."

"What sort of message are they talking about?" asked Trevor.

"The boy doesn't know," said Darius, his eyes wide in his emaciated face "That's all Suleiman said and then the men all went back to their quarters."

Trevor Nichol closed his eyes, took a deep breath and exhaled before looking at his fellow prisoner as he sat next to him in the gloom. Darius, his clothes now nothing but filthy rags, was a dried-out husk of his former self.

"We have to trust that Marek knows what to do here," he whispered. "This sort of thing has happened before, and we must believe he has experts advising him. There is no way he will let us die out here. I know that right now it seems hopeless, but we must have some faith in this process."

Darius watched as Trevor turned slowly and lay down on the concrete on his side, he groaned quietly as he assumed a foetal position.

3

Chapter Three.

The interior of the Rolls Royce limousine exuded the aroma of expensive leather and the powerful engine purred silently as it navigated the sleet and drizzle of early afternoon in central London. I opened the file and began to peruse its contents. The material was intriguing. The Polish company, Kaminski Logistica, had a strong presence in Europe, boasting an extensive fleet of heavy trucks, a sea freight branch and an air freight division. The two unfortunate pilots, who had been held captive for the past three months, were being held in the lawless region of Puntland. Their deteriorating health was evident from the numerous photographs, live streams and videos, particularly one of them named Trevor Nichol.

The company's leader, Marek Kaminski, was a well-respected figure in Poland. In his mid-40s, he had taken over the company from his late father a decade earlier. Known for his philanthropic work in sports, the arts and children's charities, he was a family man deeply concerned about his employees' welfare.

Marek Kaminski had rejected offers to enter politics, preferring to remain actively involved in running the business and supporting charities. My potential role, if I accepted it, would involve immediate travel to Krakow to assist the lead negotiator, an ex-British Army man named Matthews. I would be present for the final stages of negotiations and if an agreement was reached, I'd be responsible for the final planning and then execution of the delivery of the ransom money to the kidnappers on the coast.

The timeframe was uncertain owing to the fluidity of the situation, but it was clear that both the negotiator and the company directors believed an agreement was imminent, signalling the end of the protracted negotiations that had dragged on for three months.

THE CHAMELEON OF KRAKOW

The Jackson Advisory Group had been offered 20% of the total ransom money for ensuring a safe operation and liberation of the prisoners.

The current ransom demand stood at five million U.S. dollars, down from an initial demand of 10 million, which had started negotiations at a mere two hundred thousand offered by Kaminski Logistica. Assuming an agreement was reached at around four million U.S. dollars, my fee, if I took the job, would be 25% of Jackson's share—an amount too significant to ignore. *Two hundred grand! A fucking fortune, Green!*

As I contemplated the possibilities, I acknowledged the grave danger and potential for death inherent in this mission. Somalia was unfamiliar territory for me and the reputation of Somali pirates was daunting. My knowledge was limited to newspaper articles and movies and provided only a basic understanding of the situation. The local population and the nature of the people I would encounter remained a mystery.

If I agreed to the job, I'd soon travel to Krakow to join the negotiator and Marek Kaminski for the final negotiations. It was bound to be a tense and demanding experience, followed by an extremely perilous mission into a volatile region of the world. Nonetheless, Kaminski Logistica's vast resources made it possible to bring it all to an end and secure the prisoners' release.

I closed the file, my gaze fixed on the grey drizzle streaming across the window. *Well, well, Green. This looks like a fine fucking mess!* It was not a decision to be taken lightly. I couldn't help but ponder Colonel Jackson's motivations. He had never been fond of me, and the feeling was mutual. There was an air of uncertainty surrounding his choice. Still, one thing was clear. I had a big decision to make.

4

Chapter Four.

The cell phone rang punctually at midnight, jolting Omar awake in the sweltering heat of the basic tin shack he had been staying in for the past 4 months. He reached for the device on his makeshift bedside table, quickly noting the incoming call's country code: +48. Poland.

Without delay, he answered, speaking in hushed tones,

"Yes," he said quietly.

"What is the latest with the situation on the ground?" inquired the voice on the other end.

"There is no change, boss," Omar responded. "I'm worried about Nichol's health; he's very ill and requires medical attention. Suleiman is growing increasingly impatient with the prolonged negotiations. You know how paranoid he is. I'm not sure what our next move should be."

There was a brief pause on the line before the voice continued,

"I understand the frustration. It's taken longer than expected, but we are moving in the right direction. I'm confident there will be a resolution soon."

"Yes," Omar agreed. "It seems that way, but as I mentioned, Suleiman is getting agitated. He has a short fuse and is showing signs of impatience and intolerance towards the situation. He is constantly afraid of drones and even thinks passing aircraft are spying on him. Three months is far too long. I fear for us all."

Another pause followed, and then the voice spoke again, this time in a more decisive tone.

"I believe it's time to send a message—a clear and unequivocal one. We cannot afford to be seen as indecisive. One of the hostages must be sacrificed. If Kaminsky Logistica sees this happen, there will be no doubt about Suleiman's seriousness, and it will expedite the resolution. It's regrettable it has come to this, but without drastic action, we risk being stuck in this cycle indefinitely. The ransom must be paid. Now is the time for action."

Omar frowned as he listened to the voice.

"What are you suggesting, boss?" he asked in a hushed voice.

"I'm saying that one of the hostages must be killed. Trevor Nichol, the sick one. It needs to be streamed live on video and sent to Kaminsky and the negotiator. This has dragged on for too long- it's time to bring it to a conclusion. It's a sad necessity, but it's the only way forward," the voice replied.

Omar sighed, understanding the gravity of the situation.

"I'll speak to Suleiman and convey your idea. I'll ask for his opinion on the way forward. I'll be ready for your call tomorrow at the same time. We'll have news on our plan by then."

"Good, I'm sure Suleiman will be agreeable," the voice concluded. "Very good..."

Chapter Five.

The snow-capped peaks of the majestic Tatra Mountains, located 100 kilometres south of Krakow, shone brilliantly in the late morning sunshine. The British Airways flight had taken 2 1/2 hours, and I had enjoyed a meal during the flight courtesy of Kaminsky Logistica, who had arranged for me to travel in first class. I had contacted Colonel Jackson at 4:00 pm. that afternoon, agreeing to take on the job. Ahead of me lay the unknown and I had to make arrangements with the insurance company for an extended leave of absence. The freelance nature of my work for them allowed me to do this. No one knew how long the negotiation process would take, but, as the Colonel had said, a resolution was expected soon, and a figure would be agreed upon.

It had been 3 days since I had accepted the job and during that time, I had been busy working remotely with the ex-British army hostage negotiator already stationed in Krakow, figuring out the finer details on how to transport a substantial amount of cash on a fast vessel to the coast of Somalia. The plan was to use a Kaminsky ship diverted from the port of Mombasa in Kenya and further arrangements had been made for this during my numerous communications with the people at Kaminsky Logistica. From these communications, it was evident that tension was running high among the senior management of the company, even though I had yet to meet or talk to the charismatic owner, Marek Kaminsky himself.

The large aircraft touched down at a sunny Krakow International Airport and as one of the first-class passengers, I was among the first to disembark. Stepping into the warm midday sun of Krakow, I was swiftly transported by bus to the modern and spacious airport building, which exceeded my expectations. Customs and immigration were a breeze, and I collected my luggage in record time and headed for the exit. Walking through the "nothing to declare" route I spotted the Kaminsky Logistica driver, dressed in a black suit with a peaked cap. He held a digital sign that read 'Mr Jason Green.'

I greeted him and he smiled, speaking with a slight American accent. He immediately invited me to follow him to where the company Land Rover was waiting. Seated in the back of the brand-new vehicle, I took in the sights through the window during the half-hour drive to the city centre.

The company had arranged accommodation for me in a hotel located on the square in the old city of Krakow. While there were plenty of restaurants, bars, and attractions within the square, my focus was on the task at hand. The driver, while friendly, had limited English and my questions didn't yield much information. Eventually, we arrived at my hotel, named the 'Krakow Central Boutique Hotel.' The driver informed me that he had been instructed to wait until I checked in and freshened up. He also mentioned that Mr. Kaminsky was expecting me at the company offices.

"Thank you," I said as I climbed out of the vehicle. "See you shortly."

I exited the flashy vehicle and entered the hotel. The interior was plush and equipped with modern facilities, mixed with a few antiques that maintained the historical ambience of the surrounding buildings. The efficient and friendly receptionist handed me my key card, directing me to take the lift to my room on the 6th floor.

Upon entering the room, I performed a quick inspection and was pleased to find it met my needs perfectly. It was clean, and cool and provided a wide view of the historic central square of the old city. Below me, the tree-lined avenue was dappled in sunlight, and I watched as an ornate horse and carriage carrying a tourist couple passed. The sound of the hooves was clearly audible and the sight of it only added to the old-world charm of the place. *Beautiful city, Green. A far cry from the coast of Somalia, I'm sure.* I placed my luggage on a low rack, went into the bathroom to freshen up, and then grabbed my day bag before heading back down to meet the driver.

I had no idea what to expect that afternoon. I had never met Marek Kaminsky, but from what I had read and seen online, he seemed to be an amiable person despite his enormous wealth and public stature. However, I held no illusions that the negotiations I was about to witness would be anything but tense and fraught with acrimony. I climbed into the air-conditioned Land Rover, ready for whatever lay ahead.

"Right, we're all set," I said to the driver. "Let's go."

6

Chapter Six.

The meeting between Omar and Suleiman took place the following morning at 8:00 am. sharp. Omar had taken a short walk through the rows of tin shacks that served as the homes of his comrades until he finally arrived at the squat mud brick building that was Suleiman Abdi's residence. He took a deep breath, leaned forward and knocked three times on the door. The muffled response from inside signalled him to enter quietly and Omar walked into the cool interior of the spacious room.

Suleiman Abdi sat on a cushion to the left side of the room, his back resting against the mud brick wall. A pot of green tea sat in front of him, and he held a thin glass filled with the same tea in his left hand. He wore freshly washed robes, some made from blue silk and the light in the room accentuated his glowing brown skin.

"Good morning, my leader," Omar greeted. "I trust I find you well?"

"Yes," Suleiman replied. "I am fine. Come in and sit down. I believe we have something to discuss."

Nervously, Omar walked over and took a seat on another cushion opposite his leader. He smiled, but his eyes betrayed the fear he was feeling. After clearing his throat and without waiting to be offered tea, he began.

"My leader," he said, "Last night, I received the usual telephone call from our principal in Poland. Your frustration with the slow pace of negotiations was shared. There is great sorrow about this situation, but we have come up with something that may expedite everything for us, bringing this matter to a swift conclusion."

Suleiman's eyes narrowed suspiciously as he brought the cup to his thin lips, slurping the steaming green liquid.

"Go on," he said. "Tell me what has been suggested."

Once again, Omar cleared his throat, briefly glanced down before lifting his gaze and then he spoke,

"Our principal has suggested that we sacrifice one of the hostages. Trevor Nichol, as you know, is unwell. We now know that he was unwell before we kidnapped him, but everyone, including yourself, can see that his health is deteriorating rapidly. It may well be that he might die. Our principal has suggested that we sacrifice him for our cause. We should take him out, along with the other prisoners and execute him on camera. This footage would be live streamed to the company headquarters in Poland, providing a very clear demonstration of our resolve."

Suleiman's narrowed eyes widened, and a frown formed on his forehead as he processed this information.

"Let me understand you clearly here, Omar," Suleiman said. "You are suggesting that we take the prisoners out and shoot one of them, kill one of them on camera to send a message that we want things concluded sooner rather than later?"

Omar cleared his throat once again and nodded,

"Yes, my leader. That is the plan. I have come to you to ask for your opinion on this and see if you would agree to it. I know the men are all frustrated at how long this has taken, and I know that it is affecting morale. So, I wanted to put it to you to get your thoughts."

"Hmm," said Suleiman as he leaned forward and placed the cup on the silver tray.

He then sat back and stared the nervous-looking Omar in the eyes.

"The idea is not without merit. Leave it with me. We will meet again tomorrow at this time and by then, I will have decided. For now, things should continue the way they are, and we will make a call to the Kaminski offices this afternoon as planned. You may go now."

7

Chapter Seven.

It was 2:00pm when the driver pulled into the parking lot at the Kaminski Logistica headquarters. The drive had taken 40 minutes and we had left the beautiful old city of Krakow, travelling through pleasant suburbs until we reached the city's outskirts. Our route took us through rolling hills of green fields, with the snow-capped peaks of the Tatra Mountains to our left. Eventually, we arrived in a small industrial town where we made a left turn into a large, modern complex surrounded by fir trees. The sun blazed in the warm Polish afternoon and the wheels of the brand-new Land Rover crunched on the gravel as we parked.

The driver turned in his seat and smiled at me before speaking. "Well, Mr. Green," he said, "we have arrived. I'll walk you to the reception."

"Thanks," I said as I climbed out of the vehicle, not fully knowing what to expect.

I followed the driver across the parking lot, up a few steps and through heavy glass doors. Beyond them, a large reception area awaited, fully carpeted with low ceilings and adorned with large pictures of heavy-duty haulage trucks, ocean-going vessels and cargo planes. It was clear I had arrived at the nerve centre of the Kaminski Logistica empire.

A couple of nervous-looking receptionists immediately stood up upon seeing me, their eyes wide with anticipation.

"Good afternoon," said one of them. "Are you Mr. Green?"

"That's right," I replied. "Jason Green, pleased to meet you."

"Oh, thank God," said the young woman in perfect English. "We've been waiting for you."

She glanced at the clock on the wall and added, "Marek is anxious to meet you as soon as possible. Perhaps you would like to take a seat."

As she spoke, the door to the left burst open and a man in his mid-40s emerged with an expectant look on his face. He was slim and fit, wearing a pair of expensive black suit trousers and a pressed white cotton shirt. His tie and jacket had been removed, and he'd rolled up the sleeves on his muscular, suntanned arms. The man had a strong, determined jawline and wore a pair of rimless spectacles. He had an open and honest expression, and I immediately liked him.

"Are you Jason Green?" he asked urgently.

"That's me," I replied, offering my hand for a handshake.

He gripped my hand firmly and shook it for a moment longer than usual. I noticed the lines of stress and worry around his eyes, but he appeared immaculately turned out, clean-shaven, and clear-eyed.

"Thank God you've come, Mr. Green, or can I call you Jason?"

"Call me Jason, please," I said.

"I'm Marek Kaminski," he said.

"You are very welcome here. We're expecting a call from the kidnappers at 3:00," he added, glancing at his watch.

"Would you like anything to eat or drink? Can I offer you anything to make you feel more comfortable?"

"No, I'm fine," I said. "I ate on the plane. There's nothing I need. I'm ready to get down to work."

"That's great," Marek replied. "I can't tell you how much pressure we've all been under."

He glanced quickly at the receptionists.

"This has been a torrid time for us all here, I'm sure you can imagine."

I looked him in the eye and knew once again that I liked him. His chiselled jaw, neat haircut and open, honest manner were reassuring and unusually humble for a man of his stature. Most people of similar standing in the world of business were known for their arrogance and temper. It appeared this man had neither of these common traits of the wealthy.

"We have plenty of snacks and refreshments in the control room, as I like to call it. Please, follow me through and I'll introduce you to the team. I want to say, for the record, how glad I am that you're here. We all seem to think that we're nearing the end of this nightmare. We're gravely concerned for the health of our employees, but finally, thanks to

Mr. Matthews, I think we can see some light at the end of the tunnel and hopefully, God help us, we can put this all behind us."

I cleared my throat and looked the man.

"Well," I said, "from what I've read, you've all been through an extremely difficult time. I'm glad that things are nearing a conclusion, and I'm here to help as best as I can. Let's go and meet the others and get on with business."

The receptionists nodded at me hopefully as I followed Marek across the area and through a door on the left. Ahead of us was a long corridor, wide with glass-fronted offices on either side, creating an open atmosphere for the company's senior employees. We proceeded down the corridor until we reached what appeared to be a boardroom. Marek paused and glanced back at me before pushing open the door and walking inside, holding it open for me.

The room was large, at least 10 by 5 metres, with a massive boardroom table at the centre. At the far end of the room, two men sat nervously fidgeting at the end of the table. Near them was a cluster of computers and an array of screens lined the wall and bookshelf above them. One of the screens displayed a timer, which showed three months, 12 hours and 46 seconds and counting. This obviously marked the time that the Kaminski Logistica employees had been in the custody of their kidnappers.

The two men stood up on seeing us enter the room and immediately walked forward to introduce themselves. Marek Kaminski adjusted the sleek, rimless pair of spectacles on his face with precise movements usually seen in men who are fussy about straightness and perfection.

"Gentlemen," he said, "I'd like you to meet Jason Green from London. Jason, this is Barry Matthews, our specialist negotiator and Younis Bader, my right-hand man."

He pointed first towards a tough-looking ginger haired man who was slightly overweight. I reached my hand forward and shook hands with him, noting that his palms were slightly sweaty. Stress lines were visible on his face, and it was clear that the pressure was getting to him.

Next, Marek introduced me to his assistant, slightly shorter than himself, with longer dark hair streaked with grey, and a pair of dark-rimmed glasses. The man had a neatly trimmed beard about two inches long.

"Jason, please meet my assistant, Younis Bader. To be honest, I don't know where I would be without these two men. They have been at my side throughout this whole horrendous ordeal, and I don't think I could have come this far without them."

Both men greeted me warmly and I shook hands with Younis. I could see the stress on his face as well.

"Now, gentlemen," said Marek, "Let's take seats around the computers and the phones for a briefing before the daily phone call. I'm sure you know, Jason, that this happens every day at 3:00pm. Krakow time."

Along the left wall of the room was a counter with trays of various sandwiches, snacks, canapés, and other food. To the right of that was a coffee and tea maker and a small fridge containing soft drinks and water. Younis was the first to speak to me before sitting down.

"Jason, can I get you a sandwich, coffee, perhaps a bottle of water? Anything you'd like?"

"No, thank you," I said. "I'm fine for the moment. I'm ready to get down to business. I can see you gentlemen are in the thick of it and I'd like to understand as much as I can about what's been going on here. Whatever I see between now and any resolution of this situation will help shape our plan going forward. I wish I had met you all a long time before today, but here we are. We have to go with what we have and take it from there."

"Sure," said Younis with a sad smile. "We're very glad to have you here, we have to stay positive."

Once we were all seated, Marek was the first one to speak. He glanced at his Rolex Submariner watch, placed his hands firmly on the table and looked at each one of us from behind his thin, sleek spectacles.

"Well," he said, "as you all know, we think we are fairly close to coming to an agreement with these kidnappers. Our current offer is 2.5 million U.S. dollars for the release of Trevor Nichol and Darius Ayman. This offer was made yesterday to Omar, and in exactly 30 minutes, we are expecting a call from him to say whether they will accept. Let's all pray, gentlemen, that they do. This has gone on for far too long, and it is high time that this is all resolved and put behind us for good."

The next to speak was the big ex-soldier, Matthews. He cleared his throat, leaned his left elbow on the table and looked at me before speaking.

"If I may chime in here, gentlemen, I'd like to bring Jason up to speed with the progress of these negotiations, just to make sure that he understands how they work in the real world."

Marek nodded silently, as did Younis.

"Sure," I said. "Please fill me in as quickly as you can."

"Right," said Matthews. "In hostage situations like this, there are many things we have to keep in mind. Number one, we must remain civil. There is no point in losing our temper or getting angry or flustered. At all times, we must be polite and civil, even if the people we are dealing with are complete animals. If we keep everything calm, we create an environment in which we can maintain peace and get our offers and messages across without acrimony. Number two, the people we are dealing with are not like us. I want to explain how this is so, Jason, if I may."

I nodded, prompting the big man to continue.

"Let's say you are an ex-Somali pirate sitting in Puntland on the coast of Somalia. Your business of going out into the ocean, seizing vessels and demanding massive ransoms has finally come to an end. For the past five or six years, you've been sitting in your little village. The nearby fish stocks are depleted and therefore your income. Suddenly, you stumble across a novel approach – kidnapping innocent aid workers, pilots, etc. Now, once you have kidnapped these pilots, in this case, you have them held as prisoners. You'd be quite happy to put your feet up and relax for the next six months, a year, or however long it takes to negotiate their release. Now, imagine yourself in that situation. You could hold for as long as it takes, and maybe you could get your figure, let's say, $6, 7, 8, maybe $10 million for the release of the company's staff. For these people, there is no rush. Their concept of time is completely different from ours. The urgency we feel is something completely alien to them. Now, as you know, Jason, our initial offer for their freedom was a mere $200,000 U.S. dollars, whereas their initial demand was $10 million. A lot of people may be shocked by that small offer, but I can tell you, from years of experience, that offer constituted what we call a starting point. It let the captors know that we are serious and want our people released. So yes, it is a start, albeit a very low one compared to their initial demand. But we have to begin somewhere, and we work from there."

Mathews glanced at his watch, then at the screens to confirm the time was correct. There were 15 minutes before the call was due to come in and I could sense the tension building in the room.

He looked me in the eye and continued.

"Now, during this conversation we have had between the kidnappers and us here at Kaminski Logistica, Marek has been the person who has dealt with them. It is him and him alone who talks to them. I'm not sure if you know, Jason, but the English-speaking member of this group goes by the name of Omar. For the past three months, Marek has been speaking to Omar almost every day. I have been directing Marek on how to conduct these conversations, and I know personally how much he has struggled with holding his temper against this bastard. But I'm happy to say that I feel, and we all do, that we are very, very close to reaching an agreement. The offer we made yesterday of $2.5 million is substantial, and it is a real and firm offer. That's why you've been called in here, Jason, because once this offer is accepted and we pray to God it is, the next step of the operation will fall into your hands. Delivering the ransom money and collecting our people from the clutches of these men."

I glanced at the three men who sat there, looking expectantly at me and cleared my throat before speaking.

"Well, thank you for that. It makes it a lot clearer in my mind how this whole negotiation has been going. I can see that we have a few minutes before the call is due. I think I will just observe for now. Hopefully, today will yield a result favourable for everyone. Thank you very much. I'll sit back, watch, and listen."

All nodded in understanding and gratitude and sat back in their chairs, awaiting the call that was due at any moment.

8

Chapter Eight.

The kidnappers arrived, as they always did, just before 3:00pm. The heavy steel door squeaked on its hinges as it was unlocked and swung open allowing the bright afternoon sunshine to bathe the interior of the darkened cell. The heat of the day had been sweltering and if it hadn't been for the steady salty breeze blowing in from the coast through the rusted iron bars of the small window, the occupants of the cell would have been much weaker.

Omar, the man who always led these visits, stepped through the door and barked orders at the prisoners.

"Hurry up!" he said. "It's time for the call. Both of you, out."

Darius stood up and approached Omar with a worried look on his face.

"Omar," he said, "Trevor is very ill. Please let him rest. His stomach is causing him great pain. Let him rest for today and I'm sure he'll be better tomorrow."

Omar's response was unyielding, and he spat out his order angrily.

"Both of you must get up and get out, like I said, no exceptions! This is a very important call and everyone must be present."

Darius looked down at the curled-up figure of Trevor, his face filled with sadness and fear.

"Come on, Trevor," he said softly. "It's important we go out for this phone call. God knows it might be the end and we might be freed soon. Let's go out and be seen."

Trevor nodded weakly and forced himself up on his right elbow, shaking his head. Darius went to the other side of him and helped him stand. Trevor's emaciated body straightened up and they shuffled across the filthy floor toward the blinding light outside.

Omar walked out and stood near the other armed men, all clutching AK47 rifles, as they had done so many times before. The prisoners shuffled to the left and lowered themselves onto the sand, their backs against the mud brick wall of the building.

Satisfied that the prisoners were now in place, Omar shouted something in his native Somali to the man holding the cell phone.

"Make the call," he yelled. "It is time. Make the call now!"

The man with the cell phone nodded eagerly, dialled the number and handed the device to Omar, who stood looking at the prisoners with a worried expression. Suleiman Abdi, the leader of the men, sat nearby, his deeply wrinkled face scowling at everyone in the gathering, his AK47 clutched in his right hand, its butt buried in the sand.

The phone rang and the man immediately handed the device to Omar who pushed the speaker button so that the conversation could be heard by all. Two rings, and then the phone was answered, as it always was, by Marek with his slight American accent who simply said,

"Hello."

Omar held the phone a foot from his face and began the conversation.

"Hello, Marek, this is Omar. How are you?"

"I'm very well, thanks, Omar. And how are you?"

"Yes, everything is fine. I'm standing with the prisoners here; they are in front of me. I can turn the video on so you can see them. Would you like me to do that?"

"Yes, please, Omar," said Marek. "Please do that. It would be great to see them."

Omar responded accordingly and tapped the screen of the phone, holding it up to capture video footage of the prisoners sitting against the wall.

"That's great, Omar. Thank you very much," said Marek. "I am very concerned for their health, though. I hope that today we can finally reach a resolution here."

"Yes," said Omar, "that is what we are all waiting for. I have spoken to Suleiman, but he is not happy with your offer of 2.5 million. Let me put it this way, Marek. We don't want to waste any more time. It has been three months now. Our demand is three million U.S. dollars. Three million, and everyone goes home. How about it? What do you say?"

There was a long pause of silence on the other end of the line, and the two prisoners looked up at Omar, desperately hoping for a favourable reply.

"I'm sorry, Omar," Marek finally responded, "but your counteroffer is just too much. We cannot accept it."

"What do you mean? What do you mean you can't accept it?" shouted Omar, his frustration evident.

"How long must this continue? Yours is such a big company; you can easily afford this. Your people are sick; they need to get out of here! What the hell is going on?"

Marek interrupted the tirade by speaking calmly on the other side of the phone.

"Listen, Omar, I do not want to have any acrimonious exchange with you. Please understand, our offer remains at two point five million. You are risking the lives of the prisoners here, Omar. Can't you see that? You're being a bloody idiot."

There was another pause on the line. This time, when Marek spoke, there was anger and frustration in his voice.

"At least I'm not a kidnapper, Omar. I'm not. I'm the one trying to sort this situation out. I'm the one offering money here. I'm not a kidnapper."

Suddenly, Omar spun around in a fit of rage. He held the handset close to his mouth and screamed into it, white flecks of spittle flying from his wobbling, purple lips.

"I am not a kidnapper! I am not a bloody kidnapper! Never, ever call me a kidnapper! I am here as a translator only. Do not tar me with the same brush. I am a translator only! I am not a kidnapper!"

"Omar, please calm down," said Marek. "Please calm down; this is getting us nowhere."

"No, this conversation is over," came the furious reply. "Our demand remains at three million! We will not budge! This will continue until we get the price we want. Our demand is final. This conversation is now over, Marek. You have insulted me; you have called me a kidnapper. That is something I cannot accept. We will call you again tomorrow at 3:00pm. For now, I'm very sorry to say, but this conversation has come to nothing. Goodbye!"

Omar hung up the phone with a satisfied look on his face. The two prisoners dropped their stares to the ground and sighed deeply. Another night of captivity, another night of horror, another night of cockroaches, loud music, and bad food. It seemed the cycle they were trapped in would never end, and they would never escape.

"Get up now, both of you!" shouted Omar, his mood clearly darkened by the conversation.

"Get up and get back into your cell," he shouted. "What the hell is wrong with your boss? Does he not understand? Can he not afford a simple three million for your release? Is he such a cheapskate?"

Trevor sat weakly against the wall while Darius stood up and helped him up by holding him under his arms. They shuffled forlornly back into the stuffy, dark space behind the door. As he put Trevor down in his usual spot, they heard the creaking of the heavy steel hinges and the rattle of the heavy locks as they were enclosed in their darkened piece of hell for yet another night.

9

Chapter Nine.

The atmosphere in the boardroom was so tense you could cut it with a knife. My eyes were drawn to Marek, who sat with clenched fists on the desk. I watched the muscles in his square jaw pulsing with anger. *Jesus, that wasn't what I expected.* The exchange with the man they called Omar had been angry and heated, but it was clear that Marek had done his best to remain calm during it. However, it was obvious that we were dealing with unstable characters and there was no way they were going to budge.

In my mind, I questioned the logic behind maintaining such a low offer for the release of the prisoners. *Surely it would be far easier to just pay more.* Still, trust had been placed in the hands of the ex-army man Matthews and the two men from Kaminski Logistica were following his instructions precisely. Frustration was also etched on the faces of Younis and Matthews. I could see that the past three months had taken a toll on everyone, and the failed negotiation had left them sitting there in stunned silence.

Matthews was the first to speak.

"Well," he said quietly, "that didn't go as well as we had hoped."

"No," replied Younis, looking nervously at Marek. "God, these people are complete lunatics."

Marek Kaminski took a deep breath and slowly wiped his right hand across his forehead. It seemed like a gesture of defeat, but I could see the steely determination on his face. The lines of stress were clearly evident, and it appeared that he had acquired a fair share of grey hair at his temples due to the ordeal.

"Yes," said Marek, breaking the silence, "I guess it's another 24 hours before we try again."

He glanced at me, and I raised my eyebrows in resignation before he spoke again.

"Well, Jason," he said, "I think you're familiar with our work surroundings here and what we've been dealing with for the past three months. I don't see that there's anything for us to do here this afternoon, apart from a short briefing which will be emailed to us by Younis on the plan for tomorrow. With that in mind, I wonder if you would like to accompany me back to my home. My wife is preparing some dinner, and it seems to be a beautiful day outside. We could sit in the garden and discuss."

The offer came unexpectedly, but I had no objection. *Why not, Green? Get to know the guy more.*

"Sure," I replied immediately, "I'd like that."

Marek began again.

"Of course, Younis and Barry, you're both welcome to come along. It might do us some good to have some time away from this boardroom and a little bit of space to talk freely over a glass of wine or a beer."

Younis was the first to respond and nodded before speaking.

"Yes, I'll be there."

Matthews was the one to speak next and declined the offer.

"I'm sorry, gentlemen. I have an urgent call with my wife who is travelling to Krakow to be with me for one week tomorrow. She's bringing my two kids, so I need to go back and speak with her on the phone from my hotel and make some last-minute arrangements."

"Of course," said Marek, "it's great that your family is joining you here. I'm only sorry they couldn't come until now. This has dragged on for way too long."

Matthews spoke again, and there was determination in his eyes.

"Marek, Younis, Jason, you have to believe we are coming towards the end of this. Soon, it will be over. I know from years of experience that these bastards are reaching the point where they would rather take the money and run. I feel confident that within the next few days, at the latest in the next week, we will have a result and we can go ahead and return your employees to their families. Please, trust in the process..."

Marek Kaminski stared bleakly at Barry Matthews, fixed his jaw, and nodded resignedly.

"Well," he said with a sigh, "let us pray that this is the case."

With that, Marek stood up, smoothed his shirt on his chest and walked over to a sideboard where his suit hanger stood. He removed his jacket and tie, hanging them neatly over his left arm before turning to me to speak.

"Jason, would you like to ride with me? My house is on the outskirts of Krakow, and it would be an opportunity for us to talk. Younis, I will see you at my place and Barry, thank you for your efforts."

"Can do," I replied.

"Great," he replied with a pained smile on his face. "Let's head through, say goodbye to the ladies at the reception and I will dismiss the driver. My house is close to Krakow, so we can get you a taxi back to your hotel once dinner is finished."

With that, I stood up from my chair, nodded at the other two men and followed Marek as he headed towards the heavy glass door of the boardroom.

The drive from the small town of Wyzwolenia to the home of Marek Kaminski took thirty minutes. Marek drove the brand-new Mercedes 500 SLS with control and precision, never once breaking the speed limit. I studied him out of the corner of my eye as he drove and soon came to the conclusion that my initial impressions of him were correct.

He was an astute and likeable man who had found himself in charge of a very large company which his father had built up. Despite the great pressure of all of this, he appeared to be grounded and easy to be around, exuding an air of honesty, neatness and practicality. It was also clear he loved his family as there was a small plaque on the dashboard of his car with a picture of his two young kids and wife. *Seems a good bloke, Green. Trustworthy as well.*

We spoke openly and calmly during the journey, and he pointed out several landmarks and points of interest on the horizon, including the Tatra Mountains, which the driver who had brought me to the head office had failed to mention. I found him affable and pleasant to be around. It struck me as quite outlandish that such a likeable young businessman should be burdened with such terrible circumstances as having his employees kidnapped in some far-flung corner of Africa. *Shit happens, Green. Shit happens.*

Just before arriving at the city of Krakow, Marek took a right turn and entered what appeared to be an extremely affluent suburb lined with trees and wide avenues. The gardens were huge, and the properties were surrounded by vast walls and picket fences. There was no doubt this was a wealthy suburb and had obviously been his choice of residence with his young family.

Eventually, we turned right at a tall brick wall and Marek pushed a button on a fob on his key ring. A black electric gate slid open slowly and the tyres of the expensive Mercedes sedan scrunched on the gravel driveway as we drove in. The driveway wound its way through a series of sculpted trees, surrounded by emerald green lawns until eventually, we came up a small hillock to a large and imposing building at the top.

The house was large and modern, although it had been built using the same stone that had been used to construct many of the older buildings in Krakow. I guessed that this was to blend into the surroundings but compared to most London houses, in the bright afternoon sunshine, it was a huge mansion and almost certainly one that had cost a lot of money.

Marek parked the Mercedes, turned to me, smiled and spoke.

"Well, Jason," he said, "Welcome to my home. Please come in and meet the family."

We climbed out of the car, and I could see that the pressure had somehow dropped, and his state of mind had begun to calm having left the confines of the boardroom and the negotiations. As we approached the front door, which was a large arched affair made of solid oak, two young kids, both below 10 years old, burst out of the door and ran towards their father, shouting in glee at his return home. Marek greeted them in Polish and stooped down to hug them both. I stood there, watching the interaction.

I needed to look up when Marek's wife appeared in the doorway. In her mid-thirties, she was a strikingly beautiful woman with dark brown skin, high cheekbones and bright blue eyes. I imagined that she might have some distant Arab or North African ancestry. She stood at just under 6 ft tall. She leaned her left arm on the rim of the door and smiled as she watched her kids embrace their father. But soon, her eyes turned to me and suddenly I was engulfed in a warm smile.

"Hi, you must be Jason Green from London," she said in perfect English.

"That's right," I replied. "Pleased to meet you."

"Welcome, welcome," she said. "I'm Andrea. Come on in. I've set up a table out on the veranda for you so you can relax."

Marek stood up and shooed his children back into the house before giving me a friendly pat on the back and nodding towards the door.

"Come in, Jason. Let's go and unwind."

The interior of the house was modern and exquisitely furnished with a sunken lounge and a large kitchen to the right of the hallway. A grand set of stairs led upstairs to the bedrooms and other rooms. We walked through the large sunken lounge out towards a massive set of bay windows. Beyond them was a paved patio that must have been the size of a tennis court.

Marek slid the wide bay windows open on silent bearings and we stepped out into the warm, hazy sunshine of the Krakow afternoon. Ahead of us was a gazebo with a table and chairs underneath. Next to it stood a BBQ, already smoking with charcoal. There was a small bar and Marek led me directly to it, where he opened the fridge and pulled out a couple of cans.

"Have you tried a Polish beer yet, Jason?" he asked.

"Not yet" I replied. "In fact, this is my first time in Poland."

"Well," he said with a smile, "try this. I'm sure you'll like it."

We cracked open the beers and I was immediately struck by the beauty of the surroundings and the calm and friendly nature of the family I found myself visiting. This was a far cry from what I had expected. Yes, there had been the tense exchange in the boardroom, but it appeared that we had left that behind, and the young millionaire valued and treasured his family time and was able to separate his business life from it without letting either affect the other.

Marek cocked his head towards the far end of the veranda and motioned for me to follow him. Sipping the beer, we took a stroll to the edge of the veranda and looked down at the rolling vista of his garden, the manicured lawns, ponds and trees that lay within it. Beyond the boundary of the garden in the distance on the horizon, the snow-capped peaks of the Tatra Mountains cut a jagged line. The sun was warm on my skin, and I was feeling pleasantly tired and more than a little hungry.

"Beautiful place you have here," I said quietly.

"Yes," he said. "We are very fortunate."

I watched as Marek took a deep breath and stared out wistfully at the mountains.

"You know, Jason, sometimes I have to wonder. None of us have any clue what we're going to be handed in life. Now, in my situation, of course, I was lucky, and my late father, God bless him, left me his company and now I'm the one running it. But to be honest, if I can speak openly with you, I would much rather live a simpler life and follow my own interests, which are working with charities and sports for children. The world of business is something that, I suppose, comes naturally to me, probably something I inherited from my father. But for me, there's only one thing that's important in my life and that's family. My wife, my kids, they're all that matter."

There was a moment of silence as we stared out at the mountains. *You are in this situation regardless. It must be dealt with.*

"This whole thing with my pilots has affected us deeply. I do my very best to keep it separate, not to bring it with me when I come home after work, not to let my kids know about it or let them know that something is worrying me."

"Must be pretty difficult," I said quietly.

He turned to me with a serious look on his face and spoke.

"It is. In fact, it's taxing on my marriage, taxing on my health. I don't know if you noticed, but the hair on my temples is going grey because of it. I feel defenceless. I feel as if there's nothing I can do. The urge is to strike out and react with anger, but I cannot. I just feel so helpless."

"Hmm," I said. "I can see that Matthews' methods have frustrated you. It was obvious back in the boardroom. But he is an expert in these things."

"Yes, yes, you're right," said Marek "Of course, we have to go with the expert. He has been involved in these kinds of negotiations for many, many years and he knows the best way to deal with them. But my people out there in Somalia, they're suffering. They are starving and one of them is gravely ill. I don't care if we must pay ten million. I would happily pay ten million to get them out tomorrow morning. But no, we have to go with what Barry is saying."

"I think it's probably best…" I said quietly.

"It's killing me, Jason," he replied. "You know, the company is more than wealthy enough to pay ten or twenty million just to get them out. All I want is for our people to be freed and to get home to their families where they belong. There is nothing more important to me when it comes to work than the welfare of my employees. This is an absolute nightmare and it's killing me."

"Yup," I said, looking out at the mountains, taking another sip of the beer, "I suppose we can only hope for a swift conclusion to it all."

The two of us stood there in silence, sipping beer, until Marek heard something behind us and we turned to see Younis had arrived. The younger man had changed clothes and was now wearing jeans and a T-shirt. In his left hand, he clutched a six-pack of beer and was making his way towards the gazebo in the centre of the patio.

"Younis!" shouted Marek. "Dump the beers in the fridge and bring one over and join us."

Younis raised his left hand in acknowledgement and did as instructed. For the next half-hour, the three of us stood in the late afternoon sunshine, sipping beer and talking quietly as we stared out at the beautiful vista that lay ahead of us, with the majestic Tatra Mountains in the distance.

10

Chapter Ten.

Trevor Nichol pushed himself up from his foetal position, his back against the unforgiving wall, his head drooping low. Once he settled into a somewhat comfortable position, he mustered the strength to call out faintly for Darius to join him for their nightly discussion. The sweltering heat of the afternoon had taken its toll on them both and the disappointment from the call to Kaminsky Logistica's head office weighed heavily on their minds.

As Darius joined him, Trevor lifted his gaze to the slender beams of moonlight streaming in through the small window's bars above.

"I believe we've made some progress today," he whispered.

"Progress?" Darius responded, a surprised expression on his face. "If anything, it was a disaster, Trevor. Didn't you see how Omar reacted? Things are growing more tense by the day. I don't think there's been any progress at all."

"That's precisely what I mean," Trevor added weakly. "Marek is slowly eroding their resistance and inching towards a point in the negotiations where Omar and Suleiman will find the terms acceptable. Unfortunately, we've been the pawns in this game, unable to influence it in any way. We've suffered greatly, but we must acknowledge that there's nothing we can do to change it. As I've said before, we must trust that Marek knows what he's doing."

There was a long pause and a drop of sweat trickled down Trevor's nose.

"This situation must have garnered international attention by now," he whispered. "It's a grave incident and we all know how much Marek values his employees, which includes us. It's inconceivable to think he'd abandon us here. We know the man personally. We know he cares deeply for his staff. We have to believe that this ordeal will come to an end sooner rather than later."

Darius closed his eyes, his face reflecting the weariness of their captivity.

"Oh God, Trevor," he whispered, "I hope you're right. I don't know how much longer either of us can endure this."

Trevor gently nudged his co-pilot's leg, trying to lift his gaze.

"Keep the faith," he said quietly. "Trust in the process. We're going to make it out of here. We will go home to our families. It's inevitable."

There was another long pause as the two men contemplated their situation, but it was Trevor who broke the silence once again.

"I'm feeling exhausted and weak. I think I'll rest for a while if that's alright with you. The boy will be here later. Wake me up when he arrives and ask if he's heard any updates."

"Of course," Darius assured him "I'll bring you your food and water as well."

With those final words, Trevor eased himself down onto the filthy concrete surface of the cell. Slowly, he rolled on his side, letting out a soft groan as he assumed his familiar position, ready to endure another night in the jaws of hell.

11

Chapter Eleven.

The phone rang, as it always did, precisely at the stroke of midnight. Omar reached for the device, briefly recognizing the caller's number and country code. Poland. He answered and brought the phone to his ear.

"Hello," a voice on the other end said. "Omar, can you hear me?"

"Yes, boss," replied Omar. "I hear you."

"What's the news today? What's your update?"

"Unfortunately," Omar responded, "there is no update, boss. Everything remains the same. I'll have Suleiman's decision by 8:00 am. Somalia time tomorrow, and I'll message you immediately as to whether we proceed with the plan or not."

There was a momentary pause, and then the voice continued, a note of urgency in its tone.

"Time is running short, Omar," it said. "We must make Suleiman accept this idea. It's the only way to expedite the situation and bring this thing to an end. We both know that Nichol's life hangs by a thread, it's doubtful if he'll survive another two weeks. I've made my decision, and this plan is the way forward. It's up to you to convince Suleiman that this is the best course of action. He will agree, of course..."

Omar took a deep breath, wiping the sweat from his brow. The confines of his tin shack were stifling, even at this late hour. He swallowed audibly before continuing,

"I'm confident Suleiman will see the reason in this, boss. Either way, I'll message you in the morning and you'll know what to expect."

"Thank you, Omar," said the voice. "I'll be waiting for your message tomorrow morning. Goodbye..."

With that, the call ended, leaving Omar alone in the stinking, humid darkness of his makeshift hut. A critical decision had been made and the weight of their high-stakes plan was heavy on his shoulders.

12

CHAPTER TWELVE.

Marek's wife and kids had thought it best to leave us three men to our conversation and barbecue. Although the lovely woman occasionally came out to ensure everything was all right and deliver the meat and salads, she made a conscious effort to keep a low profile, allowing us to talk at ease.

I found the company of both Marek and Younis to be pleasant and easy going. In fact, I grew equally fond of the younger Younis as I did of Marek. It was almost unbelievable that these two mild-mannered men were grappling with such a dire situation. Nevertheless, it was evident they were handling it with professionalism and care. As much as we tried to steer our discussions toward other topics, inevitably, we found ourselves returning to the subject of the kidnapped employees.

Our dinner consisted of marinated steak, Polish sausage, a salad with walnuts, cheese, and various seeds, all topped with a delicious homemade dressing from Marek's wife. By around 7:30 we had finished our meal and I noticed both Marek and Younis yawning.

"Well, gentlemen, I think I better head back to my hotel," I said. "Thanks for a nice evening. It's given me much greater clarity on the situation moving forward. I'll see you both tomorrow morning."

"That's fine, Jason," Marek responded. "My driver will be there to pick you up at 8:30 and we'll meet in the boardroom at 9:00. Barry will be there, and I know you both have a mountain of prep work to do for when we finally reach an agreement with these bastards."

"Of course," I replied. "I'll be there, and we'll get started on that. I want to be available for the phone call at 3:00pm. as well. Let's hope it goes more smoothly than today's."

"Hmm," Younis chimed in, shaking his head. "Yes, let's hope and pray,"

"Alright," Marek continued, picking up his phone. "I'll arrange an Uber for you. We'll wait for it at the front in the car park."

"Sounds good," I said. "Let's go."

We all stood up simultaneously and headed back into the grand house. Marek's wife and kids had already retreated upstairs and the three of us made our way back through the giant lounge, through the hall and out to the parking lot.

By then, dusk had fallen, and the air had cooled noticeably. As the Uber arrived promptly, Marek opened the gate using his phone app. The black vehicle's wheels crunched on the gravel driveway as I said goodbye to my hosts and climbed into the back seat.

The driver's English was limited, so the journey back to the hotel passed in silence. I used the time to reflect on the afternoon spent with my new employers. They seem like good people, Green. All of them family men. *All of them clearly want a resolution to all of this. It's a pity Matthews didn't make it this evening as you could've gotten to know him a bit better. Still, there'll be time for that in the coming days. So far, so good. You continue with your observation and prep work and let's hope that a deal is made, and you can get the job done. Simple as that.* Once again, with the pleasant streets and leafy suburbs of Krakow flashing by the window, it felt surreal that these men were embroiled in such a dire situation. Fatigue had set in and all I yearned for was to return to the hotel, gather my thoughts and unwind. *Tomorrow's another day, Green. You need to face it with a fresh perspective.*

The drive to Krakow's city centre was smooth at that hour. I gazed at the charming trams and historic buildings that whizzed past us. Upon arriving at the hotel, I noticed a small café-bar next door, surrounded by lush greenery. Soft music wafted from inside and I decided to have one last beer before retiring to my room. The outside area permitted smoking, so I hurried to the bar, ordered a cold beer and settled down in the garden to drink it.

As I sipped my beer and smoked, my mind buzzed with a multitude of thoughts. It took some time to process everything that had transpired since my meeting with Colonel Jackson. Everything had happened so fast. If negotiations were to reach a fruitful conclusion, I needed to be extremely cautious, fully prepared and keep my wits about me for the mission that lay ahead.

THE CHAMELEON OF KRAKOW

The beer was cold and refreshing and I was pleasantly tired. I crushed out the cigarette in the nearby ashtray, downed the last of my beer and made my way back to the hotel. After checking my emails, I took a quick shower and lay down on the bed. With my hands clasped behind my head, I watched television for no more than five minutes before my eyelids grew heavy and I drifted into a deep, dreamless sleep.

13

Chapter Thirteen.

An extremely worried Omar made his way down the dusty track, passing through the rows of tin shacks, and heading towards Suleiman's house. All night, he had been fretting and worrying, hoping that Suleiman had seen the sense in the suggestion he had made the previous day. For the past three months, he had been working as an interpreter, an integral part of the gang of kidnappers. Deep down, he yearned to escape from this life and reunite with his family in Mogadishu. The heated sea air played havoc with his sinuses. The camp he had been staying in was filthy and the constant music and unruly behaviour of his comrades grated on his nerves.

If Suleiman were to accept this new plan, Omar was confident that Kaminski Logistica would finally come to their senses and send the demanded ransom immediately. Then he would finally be paid and could at last leave the desolate hell hole that was Puntland. With great trepidation, he approached the front of the mud-brick building, quietly knocking on the door three times. The muffled response from inside was as usual and Omar gently pushed the door open, entering without a sound.

Suleiman Abdi sat in his usual spot on the left, sipping tea, as he did every morning at 8:00 am.

"Good morning, my leader," said Omar.

Suleiman raised his eyes from his tea and gestured for Omar to sit. Without being offered tea, Omar smiled, cleared his throat and spoke,

"My leader, as agreed, I have come to discuss the plan I suggested yesterday. Our principal in Poland believes it is the best way forward. I've come to get your decision on whether this plan will proceed."

THE CHAMELEON OF KRAKOW

Suleiman Abdi scrutinized Omar suspiciously. His gaunt features were a deep charcoal black, and his wrinkled cheeks were like parchment. He reached his bony hand forward, placing his tea on the silver tray before speaking.

"I've been pondering your suggestion since yesterday, Omar. I also witnessed the frustrating interaction between you and the people at Kaminski during yesterday's phone call. I share our principal's frustration with the slow negotiations, and I've decided that the plan to eliminate one of the hostages should proceed. Set it for this afternoon, at the usual time. All our men will be there, but I want this to be a surprise. Don't tell them anything. Make sure one of our men films the afternoon's events. You will take the sick hostage aside and instruct the other pilot, Darius, to kill Trevor Nichol."

There was a long pause and then Suleiman's voice hardened.

"We need to send a strong message to these infidel pigs. He will have no choice but to kill his copilot in the live video stream to Poland. Failure to follow these instructions will result in Darius being shot himself. We must ensure that everything that transpires this afternoon is recorded and beamed directly to Poland. There can be no more time wasted. This afternoon, we will show them that it is I who holds the cards. This afternoon, they will realize it is time to pay Suleiman Abdi. Go now, Omar. Don't say a word to any of the men. I will see you at 3:00pm for our usual phone call, but this time, it will be slightly different..."

14

CHAPTER FOURTEEN.

I WOKE UP AT 6:00am, sat up, stretched and immediately prepared a cup of coffee. As I sipped the hot brew, I walked over to the window to gaze at the early morning sunshine casting its warm glow on the charming old buildings of Krakow's Old Town. Unlike most modern hotel rooms, I could open the window and let the fresh morning air in, even though I knew it went against the hotel's rules. I lit a cigarette, holding it outside the window, as my thoughts drifted back to the previous day and the three individuals I had met.

Marek Kaminski, a dynamic young businessman and a family man, struck me as thoroughly likeable. His assistant, Younis Bader, was equally pleasant. It was evident that both were deeply affected by the trauma of the kidnapping and the prolonged negotiations. My mind also wandered to Barry Matthews, the British ex-army man. He was the no-nonsense, get-the-job-done type, a trait that had been abundantly apparent in our meeting the previous day.

Sipping my coffee, I reflected that dealing with these three individuals would likely be problem-free. All of them were amiable and I felt that Matthews and I could devise a solid plan for delivering the ransom safely and efficiently once an agreement had been reached. I knew that Mathews had already set out an extensive plan for this and a great deal of effort and expense had gone into preparation for this very task. *He's a soldier, Green. There will be no detail he hasn't thought about or catered for. Today you can start going through all of this with him. That'll keep you busy until the phone call at 3.00.*

After finishing the coffee, I took a quick shower and ordered some breakfast to be brought up to my room. Afterwards, I dedicated the next half-hour to preparing for the day ahead at the Kaminski Logistica headquarters. My day was organized around sitting down separately with Barry Matthews to create a comprehensive and detailed plan for the ransom money delivery once an agreement was in place. Given the distances and dangers involved, this was far more complicated than it sounded and involved an operation that would cost millions. Thankfully most of these arrangements had already been made and rudimentary plans developed. But this was a kidnapping in what could only be described as a hell hole and the situation was constantly changing and dynamic.

Though I had a fairly good idea of the operation, the task at hand required careful planning and strict adherence to that plan. At 8:30 am. a driver from Kaminski Logistica arrived punctually and my room's phone rang, signalling it was time to go. I grabbed my laptop and other work-related items, rode the elevator down and climbed into the vehicle. The morning was fresh and crisp, with the sun shining brightly and I put on my sunglasses as we set off on the 40-minute drive from Krakow to the Kaminski offices.

The rest of the morning was consumed by discussions with Barry Matthews. It was a brainstorming session, filled with the exchange of ideas about the logistics of the ransom delivery once an agreement was reached. Detailed plans began to form in both of our minds and by lunchtime, we had ironed out a framework that we believed would work effectively.

Despite the offer of having lunch in the boardroom, I decided to take a walk around the facility and eat my prepared sandwiches in a nearby park. At 2:00pm. I returned to the Kaminski Logistica offices and made my way to the boardroom, where Marek, Younis and Matthews were already waiting.

The stress was evident on the men's faces; their foreheads creased with frustration. Marek impatiently tapped his fingers on the table.

I took the same seat as the previous day and the four of us began discussing and planning for the scheduled phone call. Several times, I noticed everyone's eyes darting to the large clock positioned on the wall above the communications centre. Matthews reiterated in no uncertain terms that all interactions with the kidnappers needed to be conducted calmly and pleasantly, in stark contrast to the heated exchanges of the previous day.

I watched Marek as Matthews spoke and could tell that the young businessman was struggling to maintain his composure. However, the instructions remained clear: maintain a composed and businesslike demeanour throughout the negotiations, no matter how tempting it was to vent frustration. The tension in the room mounted as the clock slowly inched towards 3:00pm.

15

CHAPTER FIFTEEN.

IT WAS 2:45PM WHEN Darius and Trevor heard the commotion approaching their cell from the row of shacks in the distance. Darius frowned, knowing that the men were arriving earlier than usual in preparation for the subsequent phone call. He stood up and walked over to where Trevor Nichol lay on his side in the left-hand corner of the cell.

Darius glanced at Trevor, a worried expression on his face. For the first time, he could see that Trevor was shivering in pain and his breathing had become ragged. Squatting down, he placed his hand gently on Trevor's left shoulder and whispered,

"Trevor, wake up. They're coming for the phone call."

Trevor Nichol groaned as if in a delirious sleep and turned his head to the left to look up at his friend.

"I can't make it today, buddy. I'm not feeling up to it. Please tell Omar I can't do it. I'm very weak..."

Once again, Darius frowned as he looked down at his co-pilot, a look of grave concern on his face. There was a pause while he considered Trevor's plea, but he nodded silently in agreement and stood up on his skinny legs.

Soon after, there was a loud rattle on the door, a sound they had become all too familiar with. The heavy steel door padlocks were being undone and beams of afternoon sunlight flooded the dingy interior of the cell as the door swung open, blinding both occupants. Trevor Nichol still lay in the left-hand corner of the cell.

Standing at the front, with a manic look on his face, was the man they called Omar.

"Everyone up," he shouted. "Everyone up and out. We have a phone call to make."

"Please, Omar," said Darius, motioning toward Trevor with his right hand. "Let Trevor rest. He's not well at all. You can see that. Please, let him remain there for today."

"Did you not hear me?" shouted Omar. "Both of you out, no exceptions!"

Suddenly, there was a disgruntled, guttural outburst from behind Omar. Darius looked over his shoulder to see the figure of Suleiman Abdi, his impossibly wrinkled face brimming with anger. He uttered something in the Somali dialect and immediately Omar burst out,

"Get that man out now! Bring him out, or we will do it. The choice is yours..."

It was at that moment that Darius realized something was seriously amiss. This was not the normal routine for the daily phone call to the Kaminski offices.

Feeling nauseous with fear now, Darius nodded at Omar solemnly and made his way back into the cell to collect his sick friend.

As Darius squatted down to take Trevor by the arm, he whispered in his ear,

"I'm sorry, buddy, but they're insisting I have to take you out. Something's up, and it seems they're all in a foul mood..."

With Darius gripping him by the arms, Trevor groaned as he was pulled into a sitting position and then up until he was standing. His emaciated body barely able to move, he was shuffled toward the door and out into the bright sunlight reflected from the sand. They shuffled off to the left, as they always did and prepared to sit with their backs against the wall.

But this time, something was different. Before they could make their way to the wall, Omar pointed to the right and shouted a command that was both alarming and terrifying.

"Take Trevor and drop him over there!"

Feeling somewhat confused, Darius stared toward the spot Omar had indicated. There was nothing there except some plastic debris and a section of rusted steel pipe.

"But...," said Darius.

"No ifs, no buts," Omar shouted, clearly agitated. "Stop questioning me! Do as I say and do it now!"

Feeling a frozen swell of panic rise within him, Darius breathed heavily and shuffled off, carrying Trevor's lightweight frame. When he arrived at the spot Omar had indicated, he gently lowered Trevor's stooped body onto the sand.

"Darius, you stay where you are." Shouted Omar.

Feeling bewildered, Darius stood upright and stared back at the group of men.

There was no doubt that something extremely sinister was going on. This was entirely different from the usual routine phone call. Darius watched as Omar pulled out his cell phone and tapped at the screen. It was clear that he was setting up a video call. He looked once again at the group of men. Although they were quiet, there was a seething look of bloodlust in their eyes and all of them shuffled around nervously. Today was unusual. In his weakened mental state, everything was confusing and suddenly he longed for the confines and darkness of the cell. He no longer wanted the feeling of being exposed to the mad eyes of his captors.

There was no doubt, something was wrong today. There was a feeling of imminent doom in the air and Darius felt a cold, sliding feeling in his stomach as his eyes dropped to the figure of Trevor lying on the sand below and then onto the thick section of heavy steel pipe that lay nearby. *No, no*, he thought. *No, it cannot be!* But it seemed that it was and suddenly Darius knew what was about to take place.

Omar's hand shook as he made the call and put the phone on speaker so everyone could hear. Darius's body began to shudder where he stood and suddenly, he felt an uncontrollable urge to urinate despite being severely dehydrated. He looked down once again at Trevor who was moaning softly and seemingly oblivious to the horror that was about to unfold.

"What is going on, Omar?" shouted Darius, his panic now evident.

"Silence!" screamed Omar as the phone rang.

The call was answered in seconds and the calm voice of Marek Kaminski was clearly heard by everyone.

"Hello, Omar," he said. "How are you today?"

"Hello, Marek," said Omar, pointing the camera at Trevor and Darius "I am not okay."

"Why is that, Omar?" said Marek "What is going on?"

"It is with great sadness that I must tell you that today we have found it necessary to send you a message. Suleiman has decided that this has now taken too long, and he feels there is only one way to make you hear us."

"What are you talking about, Omar?" said Marek, a distinct note of panic in his voice "What's going on there?"

Omar stepped forward so the camera was wholly focused on the pathetic, shaking figure of Darius with Trevor lying at his feet in the sand.

"I'm sorry, Marek," said Omar "I'm sorry you must see this. I'm sorry it has come to this..."

A strange silence fell over the scene as it all became clear.

"Pick up the pipe, Darius..." said Omar quietly, his brown eyes burning with a combination of rage and wild hysteria.

Darius Ayman stood panting and blinking in the blazing mid-afternoon sunlight and stared down at the heavy, 2-foot length of hollow steel that lay in the sand at his feet. His body now skeletal and his clothes in filthy tatters, he was a parched shell of his former self and by the expression on his face, it was clear he was a man whose spirit had been broken. Omar gritted his teeth in frustration and glanced briefly at Suleiman. The old man barked an order in his guttural, native Somali and his thin face shook with anticipation. Omar then turned to face the trembling figure of Darius once again.

"I said, pick up the pipe," he hissed furiously. "Do it now or Sulieman will kill you. The choice is yours. It's you or him..."

Tears began to carve rivulets in the dirt on Darius Ayman's hollowed cheeks and trickled into his scruffy beard as he gazed down at the curled-up figure of his colleague. Barely conscious and severely emaciated, Trevor opened his sleep-encrusted eyes and blinked as he looked up at his friend standing above him.

"He is sick! Look at him!" shouted Omar, his patience rapidly disappearing "The man will be dead soon, anyway! Pick up the pipe! Now!!"

The other men who stood around to witness the occasion began to jeer and stomp around with rabid excitement and bloodlust as the tension built. Their gowns and headscarves fluttered in the salty wind. Suleiman Abdi, their elderly leader, stood up from the cheap plastic chair which had been placed in the sand nearby. He lifted the AK47 rifle and raised it as he stepped towards Darius. The thin skin of his cheek bulged with a chewed-up ball of khat, and he spat a gooey gob of brown saliva onto the sand as he approached. He spoke a brief command in his native Somali which Omar repeated in English.

"Pick up the pipe, Darius," he said quietly, his head tilted and his eyes wide. "If you do not do as I say immediately, your own life will be over in a matter of seconds. This is my final warning..."

Darius Ayman stooped his wasted body and lifted the heavy pipe with his right hand. His breathing had become ragged, and his eyes were wide with primal terror and madness. The jeering and screaming from the other men became frenzied as he straightened his frame and stared down at the pathetic figure of the man who had been his friend and co-pilot for over 5 years. Despite his illness, 57-year-old Trevor Nichol propped himself up from the sand on his right elbow and looked Darius in the eye. As he did so he shook his head from side to side and repeatedly mouthed the word....

'No...!'

But it was then that the older man, Suleiman Abdi stepped forward once again and held the ugly muzzle of the automatic rifle inches from Darius' head. Both Suleiman and Omar were screaming now, flecks of spittle flying from their purple lips and the sound drowned out the raucous cacophony blazing from the other men. With wide, delirious eyes, Darius Ayman lifted the heavy pipe and held it high above his head, ready to make the killing blow. Finally accepting his inevitable fate, Trevor Nichol shook his head slowly, closed his eyes and lay down in the sand in a foetal position, his bony hands covered his ears in a final, futile effort to muffle out the appalling death racket that surrounded him.

"Kill him!" screamed Omar while Suleiman and the others screamed the same in Somali.

"KILL HIM!!"

16

Chapter Sixteen.

I WATCHED IN STUNNED horror as the scene on the screens in the boardroom unfolded. Marek's neck veins pulsed visibly, and his face went from a ghostly pale to a deep shade of red rage. Younis, unable to bear what was about to happen, covered his eyes and shook his head frantically. Meanwhile, Barry Matthews, though struggling to remain calm, leaned forward in his seat, desperately mouthing instructions to Marek. My eyes darted between the three figures before me and the gruesome scenes playing out on the screens. *What the fuck?*

I had no inkling that things would deteriorate so rapidly and horribly. It seemed I was about to witness one of the most brutal executions I'd ever seen. The sounds coming through the speakers were distorted by the rabid screams of the men, revealing their base bloodlust. In mere seconds, I expected to see Darius brutally attacking Trevor with the heavy pipe. The situation was appalling, and I felt utterly helpless, unable to do anything but watch the horrifying events unfold.

Marek lost control, joining the chorus of screams, pleading for Omar to stop this sadistic display of murder. But it was too late. Chaos had taken over and it appeared that Trevor Nichol's fate was sealed; he would die within the next few seconds in the sands of Somalia. The camera moved closer to Darius and Trevor. That's when I saw Suleiman Abdi, the leader, step forward, holding an AK47 to Darius' head and screaming wildly. Darius, now consumed by madness and terror, raised the steel pipe high above his head, ready to strike his friend.

The screams persisted on both sides, and Darius's body trembled with terror. It seemed the gruesome act was imminent. Then, something changed. Darius turned towards the camera, his focus no longer on Trevor but on the raised steel pipe. Tears streamed down his face and into his dusty beard. I witnessed a look of utter desperation and defeat and a profound feeling of helplessness washed over me.

Darius took a deep breath and screamed into the camera. Then, as if by some act of mercy, he released the pipe, letting it fall harmlessly into the sand. Darius's tortured scream continued, but it was as though he had decided not to strike his ailing friend, Trevor. I couldn't discern whether it was a choice or inability, but he had chosen to die rather than harm his sick friend.

Darius eventually ran out of breath, dropping to his knees in the sand. He sobbed and the cameraman stepped back. During this whole ordeal, Darius had wet himself, his crotch darkened with urine. The crowd, once frenzied with bloodlust, fell silent. Suleiman, who had held the gun to Darius's head, stepped back. It seemed as though everyone had reached an impasse and the Somali's plan to force a breakthrough had failed at the last moment.

Then, Younis Bader, who sat opposite me, removed his hands from his eyes and addressed Omar in a desperate, sobbing voice.

"What if Marek contributes five hundred thousand of his own money to the ransom, bringing us to three million? Would that be agreeable to you? No one needs to die, Omar. Can we make that happen?"

Omar turned the camera, his hands visibly shaking and spoke to his leader, Suleiman, in Somali. There was a quiet grunt of approval, and Omar turned back to the camera.

"Yes," he said, "if you can arrange that, we have a deal."

Holy shit! The room fell silent, and all eyes turned to Marek, who paused and then nodded gravely. Barry Matthews, the military man, gave a thumbs-up sign. It was Younis who spoke up once more.

"So, we have a deal, Omar. Can you confirm?"

Omar cleared his throat, steadied his hand, and spoke into the camera.

"Yes, we have a deal."

17

Chapter Seventeen.

"Pick him up," said Omar to Darius. "Pick him up. It seems that finally, we've reached a deal with your employer. You'll be going home soon."

But there was no response from Darius, who remained on his knees in the sand, hunched over and sobbing.

Seeing that Darius was unresponsive, Omar shouted to the other men in Somali,

"Come, come here and help. Come and take these infidels back into their cell. We've reached a deal. Praise be to Allah."

Two of the men slung their rifles over their shoulders, stepped forward and roughly yanked Darius to his feet. With the wet spread of urine now soaking his filthy trousers, he was led back to the cell and thrown inside unceremoniously. Next, the two men returned to collect Trevor Nichol. Completely oblivious to his severely weakened physical state, they wrenched him from his foetal position and dragged his contorted frame through the sand back to the cell door. Once there they tossed him in like a sack of potatoes as they had done with Darius. Omar stepped forward, pulled the door closed, slid the deadbolts home and fixed the two heavy padlocks in place. Once done, he turned to see Suleiman standing nearby watching him closely. He paused as he nervously tried to gauge the old man's mood but there was no telling. Finally, the old man grunted in satisfaction and spun around, his robe billowing in the warm, salty breeze. Omar watched as he began making his way back to the compound in the distance. Despite the harrowing events of the afternoon, their plan had succeeded. A deal had been made and his payday was now in sight. A smile formed on his face as he wiped the sweat from his forehead, and he too began the walk back across the litter-strewn sand to his tin shack.

It was some time later that Darius Ayman finally regained a modicum of composure and managed to crawl over to where his co-pilot lay unconscious on the filthy concrete floor.

"Did you hear what they said, Trevor?" he whispered.

There was no response.

"Trevor," said Darius "Did you hear the end of the conversation with head office? We're going home, my friend. We're going to get out of here…"

18

Chapter Eighteen.

The atmosphere in the boardroom was initially hard to gauge. All three men sat in silence, seemingly in a state of shock. It was understandable, given the harrowing events they had just witnessed. Barry Matthews was the first to break the silence. He leaned forward in his chair and addressed the stunned figures of Marek and Younis.

"Well, gentlemen," he said, "it appears we've finally had a breakthrough. We seem to have a deal with these bastards."

Younis turned to his boss, Marek and I could see the sweat running down his temples as he spoke.

"Marek," he said, "forgive me, but I couldn't bear to watch it happen. I just spoke and made the offer..."

"No," Barry reassured him, "it's a good thing you spoke, Younis. You saved the day there. They were trying to force a resolution and you concluded it. Everyone knows that Kaminski was willing to pay a ransom of three million. It was just a matter of reaching that point. It seemed like it took forever, but we've finally gotten there. I'm only sorry it took what we witnessed today to get here, but now it's official. We have a deal. From now on, it's simply a matter of getting the money to these men and exchanging it for the prisoners. In my experience, this is the easy part. Gentlemen, we've had a breakthrough here. We've done it!"

Barry Matthews' ruddy face broke into a grin.

I watched Marek tapping his fingers on the desk as if an enormous burden was gradually lifting from his shoulders. Younis stared at him, an expectant and fearful look on his face. But then, a smile broke out as Marek cleared his throat and spoke.

"Thank God you did, Younis," Marek said quietly. "I thought we were going to witness Trevor's murder right there and then. Thank God you spoke..."

Younis cleared his throat and wiped the sweat from his forehead and the side of his face.

"Well," he said, "it wasn't as if I planned it. It just came out. I didn't know what I was saying at the time."

"What you said saved the day and quite possibly saved a life," said Matthews. "In any case, the hardest part is over. We have an agreement now. It's down to Jason and me to arrange the delivery of the ransom money. Extensive plans are already in place for this. Within the next few days, we'll be ready to act on those plans and we can secure the release of your people, gentlemen."

He leaned back in his chair with a smile.

"The end is in sight, gentlemen. I want to congratulate you all."

19

Chapter Nineteen.

Omar's satisfaction was evident as he reached for the half-empty bottle of gin on the table. He brought the bottle to his lips, taking a big gulp of the neat spirit. He winced visibly as he placed the bottle back on the rickety table beside his bed. Lying down once more, a smile spread across his face. In his mind, he had achieved a great feat. After many months of back-and-forth, countless phone calls, arguments and disputes, he had finally negotiated a settlement. A deal had been struck, and his payday was now within reach.

The clock struck midnight and as usual, the cell phone on the bedside table rang. He sat up, picked up the phone, and looked at the screen. As always, the country code indicated that the call was coming from Poland.

"Hello, boss," he said with a grin.

"Good evening," replied the voice. "How are you?"

"Well, I am just fine," said Omar, struggling not to laugh. "Finally, we have done it, boss. We've got a deal. I'm overjoyed."

There was a pause on the line before the voice spoke again.

"Omar, are you drunk? Have you been drinking?"

A frown crept across Omar's face as he realized he was about to be reprimanded.

"I'm sorry, boss, but I have had a few drinks. Yes, I wanted to celebrate our victory."

Again, there was another long pause on the line, and then the voice spoke with a tone of frustration,

"You idiot, you fucking idiot! We are dealing with three million United States dollars, and you come to the job drunk? Are you a lunatic, Omar? Is this the kind of trust we have built up together? Finally, at one of the last hurdles in this race, you turn up drunk!?"

Omar coughed, realizing he had crossed a line.

"Seriously, no, boss, I'm not drunk. Like I said, I have had a few. I apologize. It has been a big relief for me. I just feel so happy that this is all coming to an end. This has taken its toll on me as well."

"Yes, I suppose you're right," said the voice. "It has been hard on all of us. I agree. But now is not the time to make a mistake, and when people drink, they make mistakes. Am I understood, Omar?"

"Yes, boss, that is understood."

"I would advise you to refrain from drinking until the money is handed over and the prisoners are exchanged. You may think the job is finished, but it is far from over. The next stage will be as tricky as the first, although it will most certainly be a lot faster. What is about to happen is possibly the trickiest part of this whole endeavour and you cannot allow yourself to slip at any moment. There will be a time to celebrate, Omar, but that time is not now. Am I clear?"

"Yes, boss, you're very clear and I apologize once again," said Omar.

"Good," said the voice. "I will call you again tomorrow night to brief you on the updates of the delivery of the ransom. But I can tell you one thing: all the mechanisms to do this are in place, and I anticipate it will only be a matter of days before it happens. Be prepared for more. Be prepared. The end is in sight, but we are not quite there yet. Expect my call at the same time tomorrow, I will give you another update."

"Yes, boss," said Omar. "I will wait for your call as usual. Thank you."

With a dull click, the line was hung up. Omar placed the phone on the side of the bed. Once again, he lay down, his frizzy hair resting on the stained pillow. He glanced around the dimly lit steel shack that had been his home for the past three months.

Soon, this will be over, he thought. *Soon, I will be free to return to my friends in Mogadishu, and I will do so with a great amount of money in my pocket. You have done well, Omar. You have done well—very well.*

Omar propped himself up on his left elbow, reached over for the open bottle of gin and brought it to his mouth once again. He took two massive swallows of the cheap, clear liquid, feeling it burn as it went down. Finally, he lay back down on the pillow, closed his eyes, and a wide grin formed on his face.

20

Chapter Twenty.

The next six hours were spent in a flurry of activity at the Kaminski offices, primarily with Barry Matthews and me locked in a private meeting frantically putting together the final plans for the delivery of the ransom. It had already been arranged that the money would be transported in a large sealable plastic crate. With the crate under my personal guard, I would travel on a corporate jet in the company of an ex-military medic and Marek's personal doctor, from Krakow to Dubai where the plane would refuel. From there, we would continue to Nairobi in Kenya.

Upon arrival, we would immediately be transferred onto a giant Augusta Westland 139 helicopter for a flight to the north of Kenya, a small place named Mandera. This outpost, located in the northernmost easterly part of the country, would be our last contact with civilization before crossing the border. From there, we would fly over the country of Somalia to meet up with the Kaminski vessel which was anchored 100 kilometres off the coast of Puntland.

The great distances involved had made it necessary for the mission to take this roundabout route. The helicopter itself had been specially chosen for its long-range capability. Once safely aboard the Kaminski vessel, it would be a matter of time and last-minute organization to determine when I would board the smaller, high-speed boat and make my way to the coast for the meeting with the kidnappers. This would be done in the company of the ex-military medic, an arrangement already taken care of by Matthews and approved by Omar.

There, we would hand over the crate of cash, load the prisoners onto the boat and return to the Kaminski vessel. The doctor would be waiting on board, fully equipped and ready to treat the prisoners. If necessary, Trevor Nichol and Darius Ayman would remain on board for medical treatment until the transfer could be made. A massive amount of logistics and organization had already gone into the preparation for the ransom delivery, and it was clear that no expense was being spared to ensure its smooth and proper execution. This preparation work had been months in the making.

Matthews and I spent hours poring over the finer details of the plans, trying to identify any vulnerabilities in the chain. The obvious weak point, of course, was the physical delivery of the ransom. We were under no illusions that we were dealing with unsavoury and unstable characters, a fact proven during the many phone calls, including the ones I had personally witnessed. There was no doubt in anyone's mind that the men we were dealing with were ruthless and would stop at nothing to get what they wanted.

With these concerns in mind, Matthews and I finally emerged from our meeting and joined Marek and Younis in the boardroom at 9:00 pm. By that time everyone was exhausted and hungry, so it was a relief to see that Marek had arranged for a food delivery which was spread out on the sideboard. Although there had been a significant breakthrough, the toll of the past three months was evident on everyone. The faces around the table were drawn and exhausted.

"Well," I began as I took my usual seat, "I'm sorry to have kept you waiting for so long. Barry and I have been going through the plans for phase two of this operation and we believe we can go ahead and pull the trigger. With the Kaminski ship ready and anchored 100 kilometres off the coast of Puntland and the cash arrangements in place, we feel confident that we can make this journey. There's no reason why we should not be aboard the Kaminski vessel by tomorrow evening with the ransom. I wanted to say I take my hat off to all of you for your foresight and arrangements. I know it's come at great expense, but I can see that this is perfectly workable. Barring any problems with the kidnappers or disagreements before my arrival, I see no reason why it shouldn't go through smoothly."

There was a pause as I watched the nods of approval from the Kaminski men opposite me.

"I've checked out and briefly been through the list of equipment and the specs of the high-speed boat I'll be using for the prisoner exchange and am happy with all of it. Using standard GPS to reach the designated meeting point should be straightforward. From there, it should be a simple exchange and we'll be on our way back to the ship. As you all know, I'll be travelling with Marek's personal doctor, who will be waiting aboard the ship pending our return to attend to the prisoners. Depending on the doctor's assessment, we'll either head straight back to Mandera and then back on to Nairobi, or we'll stay aboard while they are treated. With all that in mind, I think we're ready to go..."

I sat back in my chair and looked at the three men sitting around the table. Marek and Younis smiled, while Matthews nodded, clearly pleased that his plan had been approved.

"Excellent," Marek said with a twinkle in his eye.

"Yes," Younis added, "It's perfect..."

"Yup," I said, "We're ready..."

Barry Matthews frowned, cleared his throat and spoke again.

"There's still a lot for Jason and me to cover. We need to go through and discuss in detail the mountain of equipment already aboard the Kaminski ship, weapons, etc, but I can see everyone is tired. Let's all eat, get some coffee and continue."

"Great idea," Marek agreed. "Let's do that. Take a break for half an hour, refuel our bodies and get on with it."

It was 2:00 am. when I finally laid my head on my pillow back at the hotel in Krakow. By that stage, my mind was swirling with a million variables, tasks, and things to remember. There was a thick file with a list of equipment on the desk which I would have to study during the upcoming journey. I kept replaying the words and instructions Matthews had been drumming into me. I knew then that it was a blessing that they had hired the gruff, ex-British Army man to help with negotiations, as he had been a vital cog in the preparation and logistics of the whole operation. My part in it all was one of the most basic of all.

Matthews' time in Poland had not been spent solely negotiating; in fact, he had done the bulk of the preparation for the operation that was about to commence. For that, I was extremely grateful. His thoroughness was a safety net of sorts. As Colonel Jackson had said, all the ducks were in a row, and everything was prepared. The time to get the job done was now.

If everything went to plan, we would be leaving at 10:30 am. the following morning from a private airstrip on the outskirts of Krakow. First, there would be a final meeting in the situation room at the Kaminski headquarters, where I would be introduced to the doctor who would remain on the ship and the medic who would accompany me on the fast boat to the Somali shoreline. We would then travel to the private airport where the waiting cash-in-transit vehicle would hand over the crate containing the ransom.

THE CHAMELEON OF KRAKOW

Extra medical equipment and the crate of cash would be loaded on board our jet and we would take off for Dubai and then on to Nairobi, arriving late in the afternoon, barring any problems. There would be a quick transfer onto the Agusta Westland helicopter for the flight north to Mandera. The expected time of arrival in Mandera would be between midnight and 1:00am the following morning. We would be there for refuelling only before taking off, heading northeast crossing Somalia's coastline, to rendezvous with the Kaminski vessel. Being an oil tanker, there was a helicopter landing pad. Commandeering this ship in the early stages of negotiations had been yet another stroke of genius on Barry Matthews' part. The helicopter would be refuelled and remain on the ship awaiting our return.

Final communications would be made during three-way calls between myself, the Kaminski offices and the interpreter of the Somali kidnappers, the man they called Omar. If everything went well and calm heads prevailed, I would then travel with the medic on the high-speed semi-inflatable RIB boat to the predetermined GPS point on the coast where the payment would be made, and the prisoner exchange would take place. With all parties satisfied, I would turn the boat around immediately. The medic would take care of the prisoners, while we made our way back to the Kaminski ship. All being well, we would board the helicopter to travel back to Mandera in Kenya that same evening. For such a complicated situation with so much organization and logistical hurdles, Matthews had come up with a genius solution. Barring any unforeseen issues, it would be possible to have the prisoners back in Krakow within four days, which was unheard of when it came to previous encounters with Somali pirates and kidnappings on the high seas. This was different and would be much quicker.

Although I had a thousand thoughts racing around my mind, my body was exhausted. There would be time to sleep on the flight to Dubai and onward to Nairobi. The few hours of rest that I would get that night would not be sufficient, but hopefully, I would be rejuvenated by the time we landed on the Kaminski vessel, ready for my own small part of the mission. By all accounts, the man I would be dealing with, Omar, had some semblance of decency and normality. If one was patient and calm in dealing with him, it was possible to make progress. This had been repeatedly emphasized by Matthews, that any dealings with him should be calm and always controlled. No emotion should be shown, and no anxiety or anger ever displayed. Despite having only been with the Kaminski men for a short time, I could feel my nerves were slightly frayed. I knew it was vitally important to get some rest, so before sleeping, I took a quick shower. Finally, I lay on the bed with my fingers intertwined behind my head, staring blindly at the plaster patterns on the ceiling, wondering what the coming days would bring. *It's a simple job, Green. Go and get it done...*

21

Chapter Twenty-One.

The call came as the sun rose over the sea on the Somali coast. The horizon had just turned a dirty, pale salmon-pink colour. Omar, who was sleeping off a horrific hangover, suddenly opened his bloodshot eyes at the sound of the shrill electronic buzzing. At first, he stared around, blinking in confusion, but then it all came back to him as he sat up. His headache grew more and more extreme, and he noticed the empty bottle of gin that had fallen off the bedside table and smashed on the floor. Not wanting to disappoint the caller in Poland, he picked up the phone and cleared his throat before answering,

"Hello?"

"Good morning," said the voice. "I want to inform you that everything is going ahead as planned. Things are moving a lot quicker than we thought they would. This morning, a plane is leaving Krakow with the ransom money. It will fly to Kenya and then on to the Kaminsky ship. The ransom will be delivered within days, and this will be done by a man by the name of Jason Green."

"This is great," said Omar. "This is what we've been waiting for."

"Yes," said the voice calmly. "This is indeed what we've been waiting for. But many things can go wrong, and I need you and Suleiman to stay calm. Later this morning, there will be a call from the Kaminsky offices. I want you and Suleiman to be present for that call. This is where the official introduction to Mr. Green will take place. From then on, there will be two and three-way communications between us. This man has been specially hired by a company of mercenaries to deliver the ransom money. Do not underestimate him. He has been chosen to do this for a reason. My instruction to you is to always remain calm and deal with him as you have done all along with us. Am I understood?"

"Yes, boss," said Omar. "Of course, I understand completely."

"Expect a call in a few hours. This is when the introduction will be made, and I will update you when the plane has left Krakow. I will keep you informed every step of the way as it makes its progress down to Nairobi and then onwards to the Kaminsky ship. The end is in sight, Omar, but we are not there yet. Soon, if everyone keeps a cool head, this will all be over, we will all be paid, and you can return to Mogadishu. Are you up to the task?"

"More than ready, boss," said Omar quietly. "I will meet with Suleiman, and I will be with him, ready for the call this morning."

"Good," said the voice. "I will call you again later tonight. It will be at the usual time, around midnight. If anything should happen to the hostages, tell me in advance. Be sure to do that. Otherwise, keep your head down, stay quiet and know that we are slowly getting there. Goodbye."

There was a dull click as the phone hung up and Omar placed the phone back on the chipped bedside table. He took a deep breath and wiped the sweat from his forehead.

Even at that early hour, the humidity in the filthy tin shack he had called home for the past three months was oppressive. He opened the side drawer and rummaged around for some painkillers, found two pills, popped them in his mouth and swallowed them while gulping large mouthfuls of brackish water from a dirty 2-litre plastic container. Next, he set an alarm on his phone for 7:30 am. Finally, with a loud groan, he lifted his legs up onto the dirty mattress and lay down to sleep off his hangover.

22

Chapter Twenty-Two.

It was 7:00am when I arrived at the Kaminski offices and walked into the control room. Sitting there were Marek, Younis and Barry Matthews, as expected. Although I had managed only three hours of sleep, I felt rejuvenated and ready for the task at hand. The extra equipment I had requested for the trip had been delivered and there was an air of excited anticipation in the room. We spent the next hour running through checklists, reviewing endless pages of preparations and finalizing details. Both Marek and Younis were excited at the prospect of making a conference call with the families of the prisoners. This was due to take place at 8:15 that morning via a Zoom call. The families of Trevor Nichol and Darius Ayman would receive the long-awaited news that, if everything went well, their relatives would soon be returned home. Barry Matthews had issued a strong warning to Marek that during the call, he should refrain from offering false hope at this early stage. Instead, he was to assure them that everything possible had been done to ensure a safe and speedy return, emphasizing the need to temper expectations to avoid disappointment if something were to go wrong. I could see that Marek was struggling with this, but he nodded grimly at the instructions.

The burden of responsibility was starting to weigh on me, knowing that many family members were counting on me to get this right. Nevertheless, my faith in the organizational skills of Barry Matthews was solid and I knew his meticulous preparation had accounted for every possible outcome, minimizing risks for everyone. Meeting us at the airstrip would be Marek's personal doctor and a former medic from the Polish army. The young medic would accompany me on the fast boat to collect the prisoners and deliver the ransom and would tend to the prisoners on the journey back to the Kaminski vessel. The doctor would be waiting on board the ship with a cabin converted into a mini field hospital with specialist equipment to care for Trevor Nichol's condition. Three months of preparation, organization, sweat and heartbreak had come down to this day. With the sense of expectation and tension filling the room, I took a deep breath as I poured myself a cup of coffee and sat down one last time with the three men I now regarded as friends.

Matthews and I decided to move to the far side of the room while the conference call with the families of the prisoners took place. Marek and Younis spoke with the families, and we watched from our side, listening in on the conversation. Matthews wanted to ensure that Marek did not offer too much false hope but instead delivered a positive message, the first one the families had received since the kidnapping had occurred. The emotional outbursts from the sisters, wives and children of the kidnapped men weighed heavily on us. Once again, I felt the extreme weight of responsibility lying on my shoulders. I glanced at Matthews briefly as we heard their joy.

Finally, around 8:45 we sat down for a briefing with Marek and Younis. The time had come for us to make our way to the private airport outside Krakow where the cash-in-transit van would be waiting with the ransom money. I stood up, slung my bag over my shoulder and spoke.

"Well, gentlemen, let's get this done, shall we?"

The drive to the airport on the outskirts of Krakow took only twenty minutes. Our convoy of vehicles sped along the highway with a sense of urgency, and we arrived in good time to see the sleek Citation jet ready with its engines running on the runway apron. Several cars and people stood around outside, including the captain and crew of the jet. Nearby was a large, armoured truck, brown in colour with gold signage in Polish. Two armed men stood nearby in uniform, guarding the case of cash which lay inside.

Before leaving the vehicle, we paused to make a final conference call to Omar. The call included Marek, Younis, Barry and me. As usual, before the call, there was a brief word from Matthews stressing the need to remain calm. As Marek dialled the number, I could see that his hand was shaking slightly. The phone rang only twice before it was answered and the familiar voice of Omar came online,

"Good morning."

"Good morning, Omar," said Marek. "I hope you're well today."

"Yes, we are fine thanks. I am here with Suleiman, and we are awaiting the news as promised."

"Well," said Marek, "we have good news for you, Omar. We are currently at a small private airport on the outskirts of Krakow. With us, we have Mr. Jason Green, who will be delivering the money to you. He will be flying this morning with the doctor and the medic from here to Dubai where they will refuel and then continue to Nairobi. From there, they will travel to the north of Kenya and subsequently east across the Somali coastline to where the Kaminski vessel is waiting. If all goes well, we anticipate that we will be able to deliver the cash tomorrow afternoon. Of course, we will be in constant communication. The purpose of this call is to let you know the status of the operation and to introduce you to Mr. Green. Obviously, you will be communicating directly with him as well. All our phones are equipped to handle three-way conversations, so we see no problem with everyone always staying in the loop. This is now where we are at, Omar, and we hope that this is satisfactory to you and Suleiman."

There was a brief pause, and some mumbling in Somali could be heard in the background. A second later, Omar spoke again,

"Yes, Marek, I have spoken to Suleiman, and he is pleased with the arrangement. We are relieved that this is finally happening, and we are all looking forward to concluding our business. I will await communication from you throughout the day. Please keep us updated as to the progress of the aircraft and the whereabouts of Mr. Green."

It was then that Barry nodded at me, indicating now was the time to introduce myself.

"Hello, Omar. This is Jason Green speaking," I said, "I look forward to seeing you when we arrive at the designated drop-off point."

'Thank you, Mr Green," said Omar. "Yes, we are all looking forward to concluding this business."

Barry nodded once again and made a 'cut-off' gesture with his hand indicating it was time to end the call.

"Thank you, Omar," Marek added. "Goodbye."

Omar bade farewell and with that, the call ended.

The four of us looked at each other with wide eyes and Matthews was the first to speak,

"That went well. The introductions have been made and there will be no surprises. I think we've done everything we can, gentlemen. The next thing to do is to go and inspect the cash in the van and have it loaded onto the aircraft. From then on, I see no reason why Jason and the medical crew shouldn't get going."

"Yep," I said. "Let's do that."

The four of us climbed out of the vehicle into the fresh, crisp air and bright sunlight of the Krakow morning. In some ways, it felt a little surreal, as I was about to leave the grand old-world charm and luxury of the civilised old city of Krakow to be suddenly whisked away into the baking wastelands of North Africa. Nevertheless, it was a high-paying job and by then, I just wanted to get it done, not only for the pay but for the safety of the good people who had suffered so much during this ordeal. We made our way over to the waiting armoured truck. Marek nodded grimly at the senior man with the shotgun, who proceeded to unlock the back and swing the doors open. Lying in the centre of the load bay, strapped down, was a large grey carbon fibre box, which was clearly watertight. After a few brief words in Polish, the junior security man climbed into the back of the truck, unclipped the top of the box, and opened it on its hinges. Inside, there was more money than I had ever seen. There were thirty sealed bricks of one hundred thousand dollars each, with each brick weighing just under a kilogram. The entire weight of the box was around 30 kilograms – three million dollars in cash, a fortune unlike anything I'd ever laid eyes on.

Marek nodded approvingly and instructed the junior security man to reseal the box and move it to the waiting jet. Aware of the serious nature of the trip, the captain of the jet and his copilot stood by and saluted us as we approached in the bright morning sunlight. I pulled my sunglasses from my top pocket and put them on. We watched in silence as the crate was loaded into the luxury aircraft and strapped down, then brief introductions were made to Marek's personal doctor and the young Polish ex-army medic who would accompany me to the coast of Somalia.

Finally, with introductions done, it was time to say goodbye. I turned to face the three men I had spent most of the past 48 hours with.

"Marek," I said, holding my hand out to shake. "It's been a pleasure meeting you albeit under difficult circumstances. Don't worry, I'll get this done..."

"Thank you, Jason," he said quietly as he shook my hand with a strong grip, the muscles in his square jaw pulsating.

Next, I turned to Younis. I could see tears in his eyes, and it was as if the emotion of the moment was too much for him.

"Younis," I said, offering my hand.

The shorter man took my hand and squeezed it before the moment overtook him and he reached forward and gave me a brief, manly hug.

"Take care of our people, Jason," he said in a quavering voice.

"I'll do my best..." I replied as he released me.

Next, I turned to Barry Matthews, someone I had grown to like immensely and for whom I had the utmost respect for the incredible job of organization and planning he had done to secure the release of the hostages.

"Barry," I said. "I think we'll all have a beer when I get back. What do you say?"

For the first time, I saw the man smile and he winked at me briefly.

"Sounds like a plan, Jason." he growled in his thick Scottish accent "See you in a couple of days."

With that, I nodded once more at the men, slung my bag over my shoulder, turned around and climbed up the short steps into the sleek, waiting jet.

23

Chapter Twenty-Three.

As expected, I spent most of the six-hour flight to Dubai fast asleep. It seemed that the intense 48 hours I had just spent in Poland had taken their toll on me, and I knew I needed to rest before what was about to come. It was only when the jet was descending into Dubai that the hostess woke me and handed me a bottle of water. I adjusted the seat into the upright position and looked at the two men who were accompanying me. The doctor, who went by the name of Mackiewicz, spoke no English. He was a quiet, studious fellow in his late 60s with a bushy moustache and thick glasses. The medic, however, whose name I learned was Alexander, spoke good English, and we struck up a conversation as the plane descended.

The organization that the Kaminsky people and Matthews had put into the trip was clear. No sooner had the plane come to a halt than the refuelling process began, and we taxied around for take-off, heading south to Nairobi almost immediately after reaching cruising altitude. I realized only then that I was ravenously hungry, so the three of us had a meal together. I found the company affable even though the old doctor spoke no English at all. Young Alexander, the medic, was ex-military and appeared more than keen for this new assignment. Doctor Mackiewicz was quieter and more reserved, but I liked him just the same. After dinner, young Alex and I spoke over coffee, and I ran through what I imagined the next 48 hours would entail. In his mid to late twenties, he was at least six foot tall, blonde and well-built with a square jawline, blue eyes and a ready smile. The mission seemed nothing out of the ordinary to him, and he was unfazed by the whole plan, seemingly unafraid and not bothered by the danger. To him, it was simply another job. Be sure he will be getting paid very well for this, Green. It was a relief knowing that I would have the young soldier accompanying me and after the brief time we had spent talking, I felt confident knowing that we would both soon be venturing into perilous waters.

After an hour and a half of briefing and conversation, I returned to my seat, opened my laptop and began studying the profiles of Suleiman Abdi and the man they called Omar. There was very limited information; only a few grainy photographs and of course the images from the many video calls were available to me. By then, the faces of both men already burned into my mind along with those of Trevor Nichol and Darius Ayman. It was clear that Suleiman Abdi was some kind of regional warlord, more than likely responsible for several previous atrocities on the high seas as well. A gangster, a pirate and a thug. It wasn't much to expect anything else from a man who would kidnap innocent people and starve them to near death while demanding a ransom. I had seen the violent outburst live on screen the previous day, so I was under no illusions that the men we were dealing with were unstable, dangerous and certainly not to be trusted in any way. I kept telling myself that Matthews' prep work and organization were tight, and every possible pitfall had been addressed and catered for. We had been through it personally a hundred times and that was one of the reasons I was exhausted. For the life of me, I could not think of anything that could possibly go wrong, barring a massive disagreement with the kidnappers. After all, they were after the money, and I was after the prisoners. *It's a simple exchange, Green. A transaction, a payment made, and goods delivered.* At least, that's what I hoped.

Still, as the afternoon sun began to set outside the window of the speeding jet, my mind began to wander, and the doubts and fears began to creep in. *You must do what you must do.* I reminded myself. *Go in there according to the plan, get the job done and get out, simple as that. Get the hostages to the doctor on the Kaminsky ship and you're done. Everything else has been arranged. Your job is quite simple—deliver the money and bring the prisoners back.* I took a deep breath as I stared out at the orange vista of the endless sands and the wispy cirrus clouds above Arabia and told myself that everything would go smoothly. The lives of two men were on the line and the warlords who had kidnapped them wanted one thing and one thing only—money. They would get what they coveted so much, but I would ensure that I got what I wanted as well.

That's right, Green. Get in there, do the job and get out, simple as that.

24

Chapter Twenty-Four.

Omar's phone rang at 11:00pm that night. He reached forward, picked up the receiver and checked the country code. As usual, it was Poland.

"Hello," he said into the receiver.

"Good evening, Omar," said the voice.

"Hello, boss. How are you?" Omar asked.

"I am well, thank you. I wanted to let you know the plane is now en route. It stopped in Dubai to refuel and is due to land in Nairobi anytime now. From there, it will be a very quick exercise and we anticipate that Mister Green will be aboard the Kaminsky vessel at the latest by 8:00am. tomorrow morning."

"This is good news, boss," Omar replied nervously.

"Yes, it is," said the voice. "I want to check if everything is still in place, and everyone is briefed on what is about to happen. Are you prepared? Are all the prisoners prepared?"

"The prisoners have been told that a deal has been made, boss. That is all. I will speak to Suleiman tomorrow morning and with his permission, I will inform the prisoners that they are likely to be handed over that very afternoon."

"Good," said the voice. "Then everything is in order. You will receive a phone call tomorrow at 9:00. It will be a group call and will include the man who is bringing the money, Jason Green. I would like it if you were with Suleiman when that call comes through, so everyone is in the picture. If there are no problems, no issues, of which we do not anticipate any, I see no reason why the money should not be delivered tomorrow afternoon."

"Excellent, boss," said Omar. "I will ensure that everything is in place, everyone is ready, and all will go smoothly. Please do not worry."

"I always worry," the voice said. "It is in my nature. I do not like seeing anything left to chance. Do you understand me?"

"Yes, boss," said Omar. "But we have left nothing to chance. I will be with Suleiman tomorrow at 9:00 when the call is made. Please don't worry on our side. Everything is arranged, and we look forward to a smooth transaction."

"Good," said the voice. "In that case, we will talk again tomorrow. Goodbye, Omar."

"Goodbye, boss," said Omar as he hung up and placed the phone on the bedside table. He took a deep breath, lay down and stared up at the metal roof of the cabin while outside, the music of the other men pounded away into the night, as it always did.

25

CHAPTER TWENTY-FIVE.

THE JET BEGAN ITS descent into the sprawling, twinkling lights of Nairobi at 9:30pm, finally touching down just after 10.00 pm. It was clear that Matthews had meticulously arranged our transfer as immigration formalities were swiftly taken care of by two men who boarded the jet clad in high-visibility jackets emblazoned with 'VIP Arrivals' on the back. Once our passports were stamped, we disembarked, and I personally oversaw the removal of the crate from the hold which was then loaded into an armoured van. Dr Mackiewicz and Alex were driven in a government Land Rover, while I rode in the back of the armoured van with a guard. We immediately headed to the helicopter pad within the main complex of Nairobi International Airport. Time was of the essence. A group of men quickly arrived to load our equipment and the crate of cash into the waiting Augusta Westland helicopter.

The air was filled with the smell of aviation fuel and in the yellow lights of the helipad, the waiting chopper resembled a monstrous poisonous insect crouched and ready for attack. The whole process took less than 40 minutes. Once the crate was secured and everyone was on board, the giant rotors began to turn slowly, the engine growing louder until finally, we ascended into the starry night. Being back in Africa was a strange experience. Although I couldn't see the surrounding landscape as we flew northwards, I could smell it and knew I was back in the motherland. It was both exciting and unnerving, especially considering what the next 24 hours might bring. In the darkened cabin of the helicopter, my mind began to wander, partly due to the throbbing beat of the engine. It lulled me into a drowsy, dreamlike state where I felt everything would be okay.

Given the noise in the cabin, the conversation was minimal until we arrived at our destination two hours later. By then it was midnight and the final refuelling process still had to be completed before we headed east over Somalia towards the coast. My research had told me that the outpost of Mandera in northeast Kenya was a ramshackle, isolated village. Thus, it was no surprise that the process was somewhat haphazard. The rickety 3-tonne truck carrying the aviation fuel had suffered a puncture on its way to the aircraft, causing frustration for the pilots. Standing guard outside in the dull light of police and army vehicle headlights, I smoked as I watched the puncture on the fuel truck get repaired. The air was warm and the sound of the crickets in the surrounding bush buzzed in my ears. Finally, the truck arrived at the helicopter and began refuelling. The pump was noisy, but after 30 minutes the job was done, the pilot signed for the fuel and we were given the go-ahead to depart.

As Dr Mackiewicz, Alex and I stepped aboard the chopper in the dim light, I noticed their wide, nervous eyes. I nodded grimly at them as the massive rotors sped up and the throbbing engine grew louder. Heavily laden with aviation fuel, we lifted off into the night. Ahead of me, the pilot and copilot worked the controls, their panels sparkling with yellow, red, and emerald lights, like gemstones shining in the darkness. Although I wore headphones to communicate with them, they spoke in hushed tones, incomprehensible to me. We had no choice but to trust these men as they steered the helicopter eastward on our journey into the unknown.

Below us there were no more lights and within five minutes, we had crossed into Somali territory. Here, the population was sparse, a condition that would persist until we left the highlands and started flying over the wastelands of Somalia towards the coast.

Beneath us was a country in disarray, without a functioning government. A dangerous and violent place where help, if needed, was virtually non-existent. The nerves in my legs and arms tingled with unease as we ventured further into the darkness. The giant helicopter pounded away into the night and the darkness was all-encompassing. It was only when the moon finally revealed itself that I caught a glimpse of the stark and bare countryside. By then, we had crossed from the highlands of Somalia into the low, scrubby wastelands of Puntland. It was a daunting and frightening sight, knowing that this was a land with no hope, where innocent souls could be kidnapped and held for ransom, a place marked by violence, piracy, war and lawlessness. Still, the helicopter continued its relentless journey through the night.

Three hours later, the first signs of dawn appeared ahead of us. Through the pilot's front windows, a pale brown line tinged the horizon, bringing with it a sense of relief.

The terrible darkness that had enveloped us for hours was giving way to the comfort and visibility of daylight. Alex opened a flask of coffee and a cooler box containing sandwiches. The three of us in the back, along with the pilot and copilot, all partook in the refreshments. The arrival of daylight seemed to bring a sense of cheer and optimism among the men, suggesting that the mission was proceeding as planned. The conversation grew livelier, and everyone seemed to awaken to the prospects of the new day, despite being fully aware of the grave potential dangers it held. An hour later, as I gazed out of the left window at the stark and empty landscape, the pilot announced over the headphones that the coast was up ahead. I craned my neck to the left to see ahead of us and sure enough, in the distance, the gunmetal grey of the ocean was visible in the morning light. My arms and legs tingled with adrenalin, knowing we were crossing very near where the Kaminski employees were being held captive. Glancing over at my fellow passengers, Mackiewicz and Alex, I saw expectant looks on their faces. I gave them a reassuring smile and nod, which they returned.

Everyone was very aware of the risks involved in flying so low over Somalia. The coastline approached quickly and as I stared down, I saw little signs of life, apart from a few tin shacks. Soon enough, we were over the water and the conversation among the crew and passengers grew more animated, as they realized that we would soon be landing on the Kaminski oil tanker. Checking my watch, I noted it was just past 6:30am. We were making good time. There was a certain sense of safety now that we were flying over water rather than land. We were about to descend onto a friendly vessel, where there would be food and other creature comforts. Upon arrival, we would be offered coffee and breakfast, allowed to shower and then participate in the scheduled phone call at 9:00am. This call would involve Marek, Younis, Matthews and Omar, representing the kidnappers.

Barry Matthews' words, constantly stressing the importance of remaining calm, repeated themselves in my mind. I knew everyone would be tense, but I also knew how crucial it was to follow his instructions to the letter. If all went well, that afternoon, young Alex and I would board the RIB and head to the rendezvous point with the crate of cash.

Hopefully, everything would go smoothly, and we would return immediately to the Kaminski vessel, where medical attention would be provided to the prisoners. If the doctor deemed them fit enough to fly, we would return that afternoon to northern Kenya to refuel before flying south to Nairobi and then boarding the jet back to Krakow.

The true state of health of the prisoners was yet to be ascertained and whether that journey would be made would depend on the doctor's decision. I took a deep breath, once again feeling the weight of responsibility on my shoulders. So many people were relying on me, and I had to remind myself over and over that this was a simple transaction: a trade of money for goods. Above all, a calm head was needed. *Hopefully, everything will go well, Green.* How wrong I was.

No sooner had we transitioned from the coastline to the ocean than a solid wall of mist appeared in the distance ahead of us. Almost immediately, I could see and hear the pilots at the front discussing it and making radio contact with the bridge of the ship. It was clear there was some concern regarding the navigation and landing procedure, as this was unexpected. However, there was nothing we could do. I glanced at Dr Mackiewicz and Alex to see if they had the same concerns but were nonetheless sitting back, allowing the pilots to do their job. It was some ten minutes later when I heard the revs of the engine change and I sensed that we were now descending through the swirls of heavy fog. The pilots were looking around beneath them while talking constantly to the bridge of the vessel which remained invisible till then. But then suddenly, out of the whiteness, it appeared. The huge 200,000-tonne tanker appeared ghostly at first, its stark red metal lines appearing through the white tendrils of mist and slowly becoming more and more clear. I leaned to look out of the side window to see a group of people ahead of the bridge frantically waving yellow torches to guide the pilots down towards the helipad. There was an obvious sense of relief in the cabin of the helicopter that the vessel had been located and we were now finally making our way down to land.

The men with the torches guided the giant helicopter down slowly but surely until eventually, I felt the reassuring sensation of the suspension cushioning us as we touched down on the deck of the tanker. Almost immediately, the pilot dropped the revs, and the rotors began to slow as the sound of the engine dissipated. It was replaced by a strange, numbing silence, which seemed exacerbated by the cloak of white fog around the ship. Soon enough, a group of men in high-visibility jackets approached the door to the left and opened it. Thumbs-up signals were given and Dr Mackiewicz, Alex and I were summoned out onto the deck.

I could smell the salt in the air and there was a sense of relief knowing that we were with friends and in relative safety. The air was humid, but there was a good breeze that was cooling on my skin and after being cooped up in various aircraft for so long, it felt good to breathe the coastal air. It was then that a tall, bearded man approached me. His short, cropped hair was black with flashes of grey. He appeared to have some kind of authority over the other men and held his hand out as he greeted me.

"Jason Green, I presume?"

"That's me," I replied as I shook his hand.

"Captain Sandy Butterfield," he said with a grin, "Pleased to make your acquaintance."

'Likewise," I said, "These are my colleagues, Dr Mackiewicz and Alex."

The big man nodded at the others and then spoke.

"I'm sure you would all like to get in out of this weather and join us for refreshments. I know we have a busy morning ahead of us."

I looked at the others and then spoke, "That would be good, Captain, but I need to remain with the crate at all times. I'm sure you understand."

"Of course, of course," said the Captain. "Goes without saying. Let's get it offloaded right away and we can move it up to the common room where we have set up a command centre. All our communications will be done from this room, and you can keep an eye on everything from there. I hope that's agreeable with you, Mr. Green."

"Sounds good," I said.

"Excellent. I'll have my men offload immediately," he said.

"Thank you,"

The next ten minutes were a blur of activity as several men approached the helicopter and began removing our equipment and the sealed plastic crate containing the ransom money. With everything offloaded, we followed Captain Butterfield across the deck and through a heavy steel door beneath the bridge. Inside, there was a set of stairs to climb, which was a bit awkward given the size of the crate, but the men managed to do this seamlessly. Eventually, we arrived at the control room beneath the bridge. It came as no surprise to see a communications setup very similar to the one at the Kaminski offices in Krakow. There were multiple screens and other recording, radio and equipment, so it was all very familiar to me. I watched as the crate and the other equipment were placed in the space at the side of the main table, then Captain Butterfield spent a few minutes introducing us to his first mate and other senior staff of the vessel. It was clear that all of them were prepared for what was about to take place, but there was a sense of unease amongst the men. It was either fear or anxiety, or a mixture of both, but it was there. Once again, I was reminded of the seriousness of the situation.

I glanced at my watch to see it had just gone 7:30am. There was an hour and a half before the scheduled call with the kidnappers. We had made good time and so far, the operation had gone on without a hitch. I was pleased I had been able to get it this far, but the real test would be what was to come during the rest of the day. If all was well and I prayed it would be, Alex and I would return to the vessel from the coast of Somalia with the prisoners and we would leave that evening and head back to northern Kenya.

Tea, coffee and breakfast were offered to all of us. The nerves were getting to me, and my appetite was somewhat diminished. However, I forced myself to eat, knowing that it was essential for my strength. Afterwards, we all sat down to talk at the main table near the communications equipment.

The wide windows surrounding the room gave an unobstructed view of the forward decks of the huge tanker and it was only then that the cloak of mist that had surrounded us began to dissipate, and I could clearly see the ocean around us.

In the distance, the gunmetal colour of the ocean, capped by white tufts of spray, began to change to a deep blue as the sun burned its way through and suddenly, a semblance of life returned to the world. This had a somewhat calming and cheering effect on the men; it was as if being able to see around us brought a sense of comfort and security to everyone and the conversation became more relaxed. But all the while, I kept glancing at my watch, acutely aware that the time for the group phone call was approaching, as was the long-awaited exchange that would secure the release of the prisoners.

26

Chapter Twenty-Six.

It was 6:30am when a loud, urgent knock sounded on the door of the ramshackle tin hut that had been Omar's home. It roused him suddenly from his slumber with a sudden shock and a feeling of dread. Omar sat up with wide eyes, his mind racing with panicked thoughts. *What could be wrong? This is most unusual. What the hell is happening?* He slid his skinny, coffee-coloured legs off the bed and quickly pulled his dishdasha over his naked body as he made his way to the door. Another series of urgent knocks sounded, reverberating through the metal hut.

"Yes, yes, I'm on my way," he grunted in annoyance.

He undid the latch and swung the door open to see one of the gang standing there with an alarmed look on his face.

"What is it?" Omar asked. "Why are you disturbing me at this hour?"

"It's Suleiman, boss," said the man. "He wants to see you immediately. He did not say why; he just said to call you to come now."

Omar cleared his throat, his eyes darting from side to side in the bright morning light as he absorbed this unexpected request.

"Very well, I will go there now," he said gruffly, stepping back into the cabin.

Omar slipped on his worn leather sandals, glanced quickly at the broken dirt-smeared mirror, splashed his face with brackish water and dried it with a grubby towel. Clearing his throat, he made his way out of his tin shack, locking it behind him. He wasted no time walking back through the rows of shacks to the mud brick house of Suleiman Abdi. As he went, numerous thoughts went through his mind. *What could be wrong? Why the sudden urgency? Is he having another paranoid episode? Had something changed during the night?*

Finally arriving at the squat building, Omar steeled himself for what lay ahead. He cleared his throat once again and knocked quietly three times on the door.

"Come in," came a shout from inside.

Omar took a deep breath, leaned forward, opened the door and stepped into the cool, quiet interior of the mud-brick dwelling.

Suleiman Abdi was not in his accustomed position at the left of the front room, sitting against the wall drinking tea. Instead, he was pacing back and forth across the room, nervously agitated and visibly angry.

"Yes, master," said Omar, "I believe you have summoned me. I have come. Is everything alright?"

"No," Suleiman barked, "Nothing is all right. I am very concerned about what will happen later. Last night, a terrible feeling of doom came over me and I was unable to sleep with worry."

"But everything is in place, master. I have been translating for the past three months now and have come to know and trust the men from Kaminsky. Even our principal in Poland is certain that everything is going to go smoothly. The money, by now, will be aboard the ship and will be delivered this afternoon as arranged. What is it that is bothering you, master?"

"Everything is bothering me, Omar," barked Suleiman in his native Somali. "I have seen and heard the flying machines. The drones! In my many years, I have learned not to trust a single soul on this planet—not you, not the other men and certainly not these white infidel pigs who promise to bring us our dues. No, we can never trust the white devils, for they only know treachery and hoodwinking the good people of our lands!"

"But master, three months of negotiations cannot be all for nothing," pleaded Omar. "At some stage, there has to be some kind of trust between us. The Kaminsky men are aware that the prisoners are in grave health. The urgency is to have them freed and in return, we shall get our reward. We are heavily armed, and they will be sending only two men. If anything should go wrong, we outnumber those two men vastly and can overpower them easily. In any case, without confirmation that the full ransom has been paid, there will be no handing over of any prisoners. It will be a simple transaction, master. Surely, inshallah, there is nothing that can go wrong."

Suleiman Abdi stopped in his tracks and turned to stare at Omar. His bloodshot eyes were burning with fear and anxiety and his sallow, thin, black skin was twitching on his prominent cheekbones.

"Like I told you, Omar, I trust no one and I fear that something will go wrong today. I fear that some terrible misfortune will befall us, and there will be bloodshed..."

27

Chapter Twenty-Seven.

Captain Sandy Butterfield placed his steaming mug of tea on the windowsill of the common room and stared down at the preparation work going on near the gantry crane on the red-painted steel deck of the great ship below. The steam from the tea clouded a small section of the window in the air-conditioned room. He pointed down at the fast boat Barry had chosen for the job that I was about to undertake. He turned to me, raised an eyebrow and spoke.

"I'm sure you're aware of this, Jason," he said. "But I'll run through it just the same. We are looking at a 6 1/2-metre military-grade Tornado rigid inflatable boat, prized for its speed and deck space. At the stern, it's powered by a 175-horsepower Mercury motor. The boat has five separate air chambers so that even if one chamber is compromised, you can still navigate the ocean swiftly. This type of vessel is used by military, offshore and rescue operations worldwide, so it's an ideal choice for this job. The crate containing the ransom money will be secured just in front of the bridge. We anticipate you and the medic will carry it on to the beach, after which the space will be repurposed for the prisoners. Once they're on board, you can easily turn the boat around and speed back to us guided by GPS. Upon your return, we will hoist the boat using the gantry and all going well, everyone will be safely back here with us."

"He chose well." I said, "Looks like a fine machine, it should do the job perfectly."

Captain Butterfield nodded grimly; his gaze fixed on the deck below. I looked up, squinting into the sun's rays, now clear of the morning mist and the warmth was soothing.

"Forgive me, Jason, but can I speak openly?" asked the captain.

"Sure," I replied, taking a sip of coffee.

"Do you foresee any problems today?"

I took a deep breath before answering.

"Well, I've watched countless videos of interactions between these kidnappers and the men from Kaminsky. To say they're hot-headed would be an understatement. Barry maintains it's an act, a form of intimidation to get what they want. But there's no doubt we're dealing with volatile individuals. Everyone knows the dangers and I'm sure you know most men in Somalia chew khat. That said, the negotiator, Omar, seems mostly level-headed and practical. By all accounts, they are as keen to conclude this as we are. I'm under no illusions about the danger, but I must treat it as a simple transaction. Money for goods..."

There was a long pause as we both stared down at the deck.

"Barry's preparations have been meticulous as you know. He's cut no corners and planned for every eventuality. Alex and I are under strict instructions to wear minimal clothing so they can see we're unarmed as we approach the beach. I'm sure you know that there are to be no drones at all. They have been banging on about that since the beginning. Apparently, this Suleiman Abdi character has a thing about aircraft of any kind. They scare the shit out of him for some reason. The emphasis has been on keeping calm to make sure the exchange is done as amicably as possible. As for my personal expectations, I can only hope things go according to plan. For the Kaminski management, the ransom money is secondary. Their only focus is the safe return of their employees. I should have them back here by 5.00 pm at the latest. We will maintain constant communication. The cameras and transmitting equipment will live stream from the time we set off. Everything should happen as planned."

I paused, took another sip of coffee and gazed down at the menacing black RIB boat on the deck alongside the rows of neatly arranged crates and bags of equipment.

"That's the hope, at least..." I said quietly.

28

Chapter Twenty-Eight.

The tension in the cool interior of Suleiman's front room could be cut with a knife. Omar, fully aware of his master's extreme unease, offered to make tea, hoping to calm him down. The thought of yet another delay in the roasting hell hole of Puntland was unthinkable and he had already made plans to return to Mogadishu with his substantial pay package. At that moment, it felt like this prospect was slipping away. Suleiman, though agitated and clearly sleep-deprived, nodded for Omar to go ahead. As Omar prepared the green tea, he repeatedly attempted to reassure Suleiman, despite his manic paranoia. The ornate brass spittoons that were positioned around the room were filled with gooey remnants of chewed khat betraying Suleiman's sleepless night.

"Now, master, please take a seat and let me bring you some tea," Omar said, eager to explain once again the day's proceedings in hopes of allaying Suleiman's delusions.

Reluctantly, Suleiman settled in his usual spot on a silken cushion against the mud-brick wall, his gaze weary but attentive as Omar placed the silver tray on the floor and handed him the dainty teacup with a tremble.

"May I sit, master?" Omar asked, receiving a nod in response.

He sat carefully in front of Suleiman, waiting respectfully as his master sipped the hot beverage noisily.

"That is better, may I speak?" Omar asked, seeking permission to outline the day's schedule.

Suleiman's silent nod prompted him to proceed.

"Master," he began, "today at 9:00am, roughly two hours from now, we'll have a group call to confirm the ransom money's placement on the Kaminsky vessel, with the cash and prisoner exchange slated for this afternoon. Today is the day we have all been waiting for."

Omar went on to reassure Suleiman of the extensive preparations from both sides, emphasizing the great lengths to which Kaminsky Logistica had gone to ensure a smooth exchange.

"Master, forgive my confidence, but I truly believe the deal will proceed without an issue. My interactions with these people have fostered a certain trust in their intentions. Despite your suspicions, these are businessmen simply seeking a straightforward transaction. Added to this we have the reassurances from our principal in Poland. I truly feel we are safe to proceed."

Omar went on to detail their own security measures: numerous armed men, the option of putting snipers in position and stressing the impossibility of being outmanoeuvred by the two unarmed men arriving for the exchange.

"Any misstep from them and surely, we will have the upper hand," said Omar, desperately trying to convince his master.

Suleiman, weary but still listening, took a full minute before responding. His acknowledgement, though grim, indicated a grudging willingness to trust Omar's judgment. Omar, now sensing a breakthrough, confirmed the scheduled call at 9:00 am. and promised vigilant oversight to ensure everything proceeded as planned.

"Now, master, let us wait for the call with patience and faith in Allah," Omar concluded, once again humbly positioning himself as a grovelling servant committed to the mission's success and Suleiman's peace of mind.

29

Chapter Twenty-Nine.

I stared down at the crates and boxes positioned next to the RIB, then turned to Captain Butterfield. At the time it seemed a bit surreal where I was standing and the speed at which events had happened since my meeting with Colonel Jackson. Everything had happened so fast, and a million thoughts were racing through my tired mind. I shook my head, drank the last of my coffee and addressed him.

"Well," I said glancing at my watch, "it looks like we have some time before the conference call. If it's okay with you, I'd like to go through the list of equipment."

"Sure, certainly," he replied. "I have copies of the full list. If you'd like, we can step over to the table and go through it together."

"Great," I said. "Let's do that."

We walked over to the communications centre, sat down and the big man handed me a printed sheet of all the equipment chosen for the mission. I immediately recognized Barry Matthews' handiwork in the exhaustive and meticulously chosen selection, perfectly suited for the job. I leaned back in the chair and quickly browsed through it.

The list was extensive, and I rapidly read through it, doing my best to memorize it all. There was a GPS navigation system for accurate location tracking; a marine radar to detect other vessels and obstacles, night vision devices, including goggles for low light; a compass and nautical charts as traditional navigation backups; a satellite phone for long-range communication; a VHF radio for short-range communication with the Kaminski ship; personal locator beacons for Alex and me in case of emergency; comprehensive first aid kits; emergency medical kits with tourniquets, chest seals and emergency bandages; IV fluid and hypothermia prevention gear for the maritime environment; life jackets for all team members and hostages; survival rafts in case the RIB was compromised; water desalinization devices for fresh drinking water; emergency rations of high-energy, long-life food supplies; bolt cutters, grappling hooks, and ropes; GoPro cameras; binoculars, flashlights and tactical lights; and finally, water-resistant bags.

Each item was justified by the mission's needs, our strategy and the rules agreed with the kidnappers. There were to be no weapons. A disadvantage but there was nothing I could do about that. The balance between preparedness, space limitations on the RIB and the need for mobility and speed was crucial.

Having gone through the list, I nodded and stared out of the window at the ocean swells.

"Barry's thought of everything," I said. "I can't see anything we'd need beyond what he's chosen. Thank you for organizing everything and getting it ready."

Captain Butterfield nodded grimly, meeting my gaze. After a pause, he spoke,

"This isn't half of it. Our tiny sick bay has been converted into a fully equipped hospital. Marek has spared no expense. It's been a big effort put together by a lot of people and substantial resources. Just the cost of having this ship anchored out here is huge. And now it's all come down to you being here today. The final cog in the machine. Quite a responsibility..."

"Well," I replied, glancing at my watch, "they're after one thing: money. And we're after the prisoners. It's a simple transaction—money for goods. Now, I think we better get ready for the conference call. Let's hope these bastards don't shift the goalposts at this late hour..."

30

Chapter Thirty.

Trevor Nichol and Darius Ayman were waiting to hear the lock being opened just before 9:00am that morning. Despite Trevor's grave illness, the prospect of imminent rescue had bolstered his spirits. He sat leaning against the concrete wall of the cell, his sunken eyes filled with expectation. As usual, the keys rattled noisily in the locks and the bolts slid open. The bright morning sun streamed into the cell from the open door, causing the prisoners to squint their eyes against its brilliance. Thousands of tiny specks of dust hovered in the diagonal yellow rays.

The mood was distinctly different that day and Omar seemed unexpectedly cheerful.

"Right, everyone up and out," he announced cheerfully. "Today is the day you will go home. But first, we must make a call to finalize things. Come on, everyone up."

Darius helped Trevor to his feet and the two of them shuffled across the dirty floor towards the cell door. Once outside, they sat down in their usual spot in the sand, backs against the wall. This had been the routine every morning since they had been kidnapped and this was no exception. But today, there was an air of excitement and anticipation among the others.

The men mumbled to themselves in their guttural Somali dialect. Darius noticed Suleiman sitting back on a plastic chair, looking fidgety and nervous. He kept fumbling with the assault rifle on his lap, something that seemed amiss to Darius, though he couldn't pinpoint exactly what it was.

It was then that Omar stepped forward, checked the time on his cell phone and made the call. It was answered within one ring.

"Good morning," said Omar. "Marek, can you hear me?"

"Yes," replied Marek, as if clarifying for someone else's benefit. "I can hear you."

Omar glanced around at the others.

"We have the prisoners outside as usual, and we are hoping that everything is finalized for the exchange this afternoon. Is this going to happen?"

After a brief pause, Marek's voice came over the speaker again.

"I just wanted to confirm that everyone can hear us. Uh, Jason, are you online and can you hear everything that's going on here?"

"Yes," I said. "I'm here, Marek and I can hear everything. I'm also watching on the screens as you are."

"Excellent," Marek replied. "Now, Omar, if you'd like to continue?"

"Well," Omar continued, "as I was saying, we are all here. The prisoners are ready, and it appears Mr. Green is on board the Kaminski vessel. I assume everything is in place for the exchange later today?"

"Yes," I said. "I've gone through the equipment. We have arrived with the money and thanks to everyone involved, I am confident that we will be arriving on the coast at the designated spot at 3:00 this afternoon, assuming there are no snags."

"There will be no delays," Omar replied eagerly. "We are all anxious to get this done. Everyone is ready for the exchange."

There was a brief pause before Marek spoke again.

"Omar, I'm very glad that it has come to this, and we look forward to a simple transaction this afternoon. Mr. Green will be with you as promised and will hand over the crate of cash. Please, let us all stick to the arrangement and ensure the prisoners are there on the beach waiting for the arrival of the boat. With that, I think our business here is done. We will continue this conversation this afternoon, and everyone will be able to communicate with each other as the events are streamed to us here. We know our people are looking forward to coming home. I want to thank you all and the next time we speak, it'll be around 3:00, if everyone's agreed."

"That's fine, I'll be there..." I said.

Omar nodded frantically, looked over at Suleiman and nodded again. With that, the line was hung up and the conversation was over.

"Well," said Omar as he walked over to the prisoners, "It seems that indeed you will be going home this afternoon. This is great news. But for now, you must go back into your cell one last time. Come on, get up. You have reason to be happy."

31

Chapter Thirty-One.

After the conference call concluded and the screens went dark, I turned towards Captain Butterfield. He gave me a grim nod, an indication of his satisfaction with the call's outcome.

"Looks like that went pretty well," he remarked.

"Sounds like it," I agreed. "If it's all right with you, I'd like to lock this conference room for the next couple of hours while I head down with Alex to start preparing the boat."

"Of course," Captain Butterfield replied. "This room is fully lockable. No one will be able to enter once it's secured and you'll have the keys to both locks."

The captain stood, cleared his throat and spoke loudly.

"Gentlemen, if you'd all stand, we can head out. Jason can lock the doors behind us, and we can proceed with equipping the boat."

Alex, the first mate and I stood, making our way to the door. Once outside, Captain Butterfield closed the heavy steel door, securing it with two thick sliding bolts. He then retrieved two large padlocks from a day bag, still in their original plastic packaging. Using a pair of scissors from the same bag, he cut open the packaging and handed me the padlocks.

I tested them before locking the bolts securely. With the keys safely pocketed, we descended the steel stairway to the tanker's deck level. Once there, we stepped out into the bright morning sunshine. The mist had cleared, and the heat was intense.

With Captain Butterfield's list in hand, Alex, a crew member and I spent the next two hours meticulously going through every item on the list, loading them onto the RIB. We first made space at the front for the crate, which would be secured with ratchet straps, ensuring there was enough room for the prisoners once the exchange was made.

By 11:45am, after triple-checking our preparations, I was satisfied. We attached the RIB to the gantry crane, lifting and dropping it to the heaving swell below three times to ensure everything was functional. Once content, I instructed the crane operator to leave the RIB attached to the gantry crane for later.

By then, the sun had caused my exposed skin to tingle with sunburn, and I felt dehydrated and tired. Captain Butterfield, who had been observing, stepped forward to ask if I was satisfied with the arrangements.

"Looks good to me," I replied. "Right now, I'm feeling a bit thirsty and tired. If it's okay with you, I'd like to head back to the communications room. If you could have a bunk brought in, I'll try to get some rest before we head to the coast."

"Certainly," said the captain. "We have a bunk ready for you. I understand you must stay near the crate of money. Let's head up there now. You can unlock the doors, and we'll set up your bunk and leave you to rest."

"Good," I said looking over the loaded RIB one last time. "Let's do that."

32

CHAPTER THIRTY-TWO.

SULEIMAN ABDI PACED THE front room of his mud-brick building, visibly nervous, agitated, almost frantic. Omar had arrived, having been summoned at midday for yet another meeting with his boss. He had hoped that Suleiman might have calmed down from their morning meeting, but, regrettably, this was not the case. If anything, Suleiman seemed to be in a worse mental state.

"Go to the table," Suleiman said impatiently. "Open the map. I want to double-check where this will all take place."

Omar walked over to the rickety table that stood on the right-hand side of the room near the small window. On the surface lay a rolled-up, grubby sheet of paper. As instructed, he unfurled it and placed it back on the table, using several brass and silver objects as paperweights to keep it flat. Omar bent over and studied the coastline depicted on the map, then consulted his phone and GPS device for confirmation. After a minute, he spoke.

"It is here, master. Allow me to show you, please."

Suleiman stopped his pacing, grunted and stepped towards the table. He leaned over and studied the point on the map that Omar was indicating.

"It is here, sir. This is the arranged spot. This is the position where the boat will arrive. This is the exact place where we will hand over the hostages and collect our ransom."

Suleiman gazed at the map, his deeply sunken eyes darting from the map to the GPS device and the flat screen of Omar's phone.

"I have a bad feeling," he muttered worriedly. "I have a terrible feeling about this. These white devils are going to trick us. I have seen their drones. They plan to ambush us, I feel it. If I know them, they have a plan up their sleeves. They will pretend to deliver the money and then attempt an ambush. It is prudent that we take serious measures to mitigate against this possibility."

"What are you proposing, master?" asked Omar, trying his best to mask his desperation.

Suleiman looked him in the eye and then pointed down towards the map and the GPS device.

"Here, there are several buildings. I want a sniper here, here and here. They must be hidden from view and must be ready to fire the moment something goes wrong. Their instructions must be to shoot to kill. There is no way I will allow this exchange to go forward without these snipers in place. Assign three of our best men and make sure to include Faizal. Instruct them on their duties this afternoon. Personally inspect their positions at the locations I have mentioned. Make sure they are completely concealed and tell them to watch the proceedings carefully. We will be down there at 3:00pm awaiting the boat and the ransom. But if my suspicions are confirmed, there will be trouble. I do not trust this man they call Green. No, I trust no one. No infidel can ever be trusted."

"Master, I will have the snipers in place and ensure that Faizal is one of them. I will make sure they're hidden and will do my best to ensure everything goes smoothly and the money is received without incident."

"Good," said Suleiman. "These preventative measures are necessary. They are to safeguard us all. There will be no pulling the wool over our eyes. We will not allow it. Now, go and arrange everything. Time is short. Return when everything is done as instructed."

"Yes, master," said Omar, bowing slightly and dropping his gaze to the floor. "I will get it done immediately and will return soon."

33

CHAPTER THIRTY-THREE.

The communications room was enveloped in silence, punctuated only by the groaning and creaking of the massive ship beneath me. I draped the eye cover I had salvaged from the jet over my eyes, attempting to shield myself from the intrusive sunlight. *Try to sleep, Green. You must try.* Despite the air conditioning, the room's atmosphere was warm, and the tang of salt lingered in the air. However, the immense weight of responsibility resting on my shoulders banished any thoughts of sleep. I lay there, motionless, mentally preparing myself, meticulously revisiting the sequence of events planned for the afternoon. The preparation had been thorough, covering every possible outcome. Yet, the weight of expectation from the numerous people depending on me was overwhelming. It wasn't just a significant amount of money at stake—it was the lives of fathers, brothers and husbands. This alone made sleep an impossibility. Instead, I lay still, forcing my body into a state of rest. *Just breathe and take your mind off it, Green.*

I had consumed 2 litres of water with rehydration salts and apple juice, trusting it to replenish my body after the arduous journey so far. Alex, the army medic who would accompany me to the coast of Somalia, was taking his rest in a nearby cabin, following my directive to do the same. The young man seemed oddly at ease, almost as if he were on some casual adventure. This puzzled me, given the gravity and potential danger. His nonchalance seemed misplaced, especially when my thoughts kept circling back to the harrowing moment when Omar had screamed at Darius to bludgeon Trevor to death. Omar's eyes had burned with a maniacal fervour, a wild streak of madness and bloodlust that haunted me. The unstable and violent nature of the individuals we were dealing with had been emphasized repeatedly. The importance of maintaining calm had been ingrained in me so deeply that it became my sole focus.

It was for these reasons that sleep was an elusive luxury for me. Instead, I found a forced tranquility, repeatedly going over the upcoming events in my mind like scenes from a high-definition film. The boarding process, the journey, the exchange, the retrieval and the return to the Kaminski vessel played out in my mind repeatedly. Time became a blur as I lay there, lost in my thoughts, preparing for what lay ahead.

34

Chapter Thirty-Four.

"It is done, Master," said Omar.

"How many men?" asked Suleiman.

"There are three men, as you requested, Master. I have placed Faizal to the south in the rocky outcrop, one directly ahead of the designated landing spot, hidden to the side of a building and camouflaged with some sacking and one to the left, among the other boats. I have conducted a reconnaissance of the area and ensured that all of the men are well hidden from view. Even if this man, Green, who is delivering the ransom money, uses binoculars, he will not see our people. That I can guarantee," Omar explained.

Suleiman rocked on the balls of his feet and closed his eyes, deep in thought.

"Hmm," he murmured. "Good. At least we are taking some preventative measures against these devils. But I have something else to request."

"Yes, master?" Omar inquired.

Suleiman Abdi walked back to the table where the map was still laid out. He pointed at the rocky outcrop to the south of the landing spot and instructed,

"This here, Omar, is one of the best defensive positions. This is because of the height of the rocks. I want Faizal to be armed with an RPG rocket launcher. This is a safety measure, in case there are any tricks or funny games by these devils who will be delivering our money. If anything goes wrong, at my signal, he should launch the rocket and destroy the boat on which they travel to our coast today."

"Certainly, Master. There are several of these rocket launchers in the armoury, and I will deliver one to Faizal immediately and give him the instructions," Omar responded.

"Yes, you do that," Suleiman said, his voice quiet with thought and anticipation. "Deliver the rocket launcher to Faizal and tell him if I raise my weapon to the sky, that is the signal for him to fire upon the boat and kill the devils who will be visiting us later. Blow them into small pieces. Am I understood, Omar?"

"Yes, Master," said Omar, bowing slightly and dropping his gaze to the floor. "I shall attend to this immediately."

35

Chapter Thirty-Five.

It was 1:00pm when I finally summoned Captain Butterfield and his team to the communications room where I had been resting. It was time to move the crate of cash down to the deck beside the RIB in preparation for the impending journey. The captain arrived, his forehead creased with worry and his complexion pale from lack of sleep and anxiety.

"Right," I said to him, "Let's get this crate down to the boat, get it loaded and strapped in. After that, I need to do a final check of our equipment. We need to ensure the streaming cameras are operational. Alex and I can do a final run-through of our schedule and get ready to make our move."

"Certainly," Captain Butterfield responded, signalling to the two sailors behind him. "OK guys, grab this crate and let's head down to the RIB."

The mood was solemn as the men grasped the heavy plastic crate by its handles. I followed them down the stairs until we emerged through the steel door at deck level and made our way towards the waiting RIB which was still attached to the gantry crane. The heat was fierce, radiating from the steel deck and the rays of the sun reflected harshly off the surrounding ocean. The preparation on the boat's forward deck had been excellent so that the crate slotted neatly into its brackets and was then quickly secured with ratchet straps for the journey ahead.

The journey of 100 kilometres through choppy seas to the coast of the lawless country of Somalia was about to commence. Once the crate was secured, I stepped into the RIB and began a final review of the equipment. Finally, I told young Alex to don his webbing and helmet and activate the streaming camera.

Captain Butterfield watched the proceedings, clutching a handheld radio in his left hand. Alex and I both activated our cameras and repeatedly voice-checked,

"Testing, 1-2-3," turning around to ensure the cameras were working.

There was a squawked response on the captain's radio indicating everything was operational and the video was streaming as it should. He gave us a thumbs-up signal.

Next, I checked the boat for its various components—fuel, power and other necessities—and verified all the extra equipment crates of medical and survival gear, which I hoped we wouldn't need. The last item to be checked was the GPS unit which showed a straight green dotted line across the ocean from our current position to the drop-off point on the coast. *Good.*

The procedure had been rehearsed countless times with Barry Matthews back in Krakow so by then it felt almost like a routine. If successful, the entire operation onshore should take no more than 5 minutes. I had studied the surrounding area in detail via Google Maps. Apart from a few ramshackle buildings and a rocky outcrop to the south, the beach was wide, with a low shelf and small wavelets.

All being well, I would land the RIB on the sand, meet the kidnappers and then immediately unshackle the plastic crate from its housing on the forward deck of the RIB. Alex and I would carry it and dump it on the sand, then return to the boat and await the hostages, who would be no more than 20 or 30 metres away under the watch of the kidnappers. Once they were satisfied with the contents of the crate and had verified the cash was indeed there, the two hostages would be brought forward and helped onto the boat.

Once this was done, Alex and I would push the boat back into the waves, climb on, I would re-start the engine, spin the boat around and head back to the Kaminski vessel. Having checked the weather report, I knew the ocean conditions were stable, and given the capacity of the engine on the RIB, we would average a speed of 90 kilometres an hour. This meant we would take roughly an hour and ten minutes to reach the designated spot on the coast.

The boat was heavily laden with equipment, so pushing it faster was a risk I was not prepared to take given the precarious health of the hostages. I would not race back to the Kaminski vessel; instead, I would take it easy, allowing Alex to tend to Trevor and Darius, ensuring their ride back to safety was as comfortable as possible. There was no need to shake them up further from the awful ordeal they had already suffered.

Once we arrived at the Kaminski vessel, I was to position the RIB under the gantry crane and assist Alex in attaching the fittings to the lines of the crane. From there, we would be lifted aboard, and my job would essentially be done. Immediately, the hostages would be taken to the sick bay to Dr. Mackiewicz for an assessment. A decision would be made whether we would return to northern Kenya, Nairobi and on to Krakow. If the doctor deemed the health of the hostages good enough, we would be leaving that evening. If not, we would remain aboard the Kaminski vessel until the doctor said the hostages were good to travel.

I found it somewhat relieving to get on with the pre-mission checks. Having lain up in the communications room for so long, left alone with only my thoughts and fears, it seemed that busying myself took my mind off the danger and the weight of responsibility.

Now, it was time to move, and I gave the RIB one final look over. With what seemed like a thousand checks completed and all the equipment functioning correctly, I looked at my watch to see it was 1:40pm. I stepped out of the RIB and walked up to Captain Butterfield who stood nearby, desperately trying to fight the nerves that all of us were suffering.

"Well, Captain," I said, "It looks like we have catered for everything. Given the conditions of the sea now, I think it's about time we leave. If, for some reason, I think we'll arrive at the rendezvous point earlier than expected, I will circle around and idle the engine until I'm ready to move. The live stream will begin 10 minutes before I make landfall. I think it's time we get going. I'll see you later."

Captain Butterfield closed his eyes briefly and a trickle of sweat ran down his right temple into his bushy beard. He shook his head, then stared at me squarely in the face.

"Godspeed, Jason," he said quietly. "Bring back our people. Bring them back where they belong."

"I'll do that," I said, "Don't worry, I will do that."

36

Chapter Thirty-Six.

The air hummed with tension as Darius whispered,

"I can hear them coming. There are also vehicles. Listen."

Trevor Nichol, struggling with his weakened state, forced himself to sit up. He leaned his back against the concrete wall, and despite his sunken cheeks and hollow eyes, a glimmer of hope sparked within him. It was a hope that today might be the last day they would spend in the miserable hellhole they had been confined to for the past three months. Outside, the sound of their kidnapper's clamour stirred an air of excitement within the cell. The prisoners waited patiently until the heavy padlocks were unlocked and the bolts slid open. As usual, it was Omar who stood at the door. Trevor blinked against the sunlight streaming into the dark, gloomy space.

"Time to go home, folks," Omar said with a forced smile. "Come on, up you get. The time has finally come."

Without a word, Darius walked over to Trevor and helped him to his feet by supporting him under his arms. Barely able to walk, they shuffled toward the door where two armed men stood, brandishing their AK-47s. Omar's seemingly false cheerfulness puzzled both Darius and Trevor. Given that the kidnappers were likely due a significant ransom, this should have been a happy occasion for them. But for some reason, Omar appeared nervous and somewhat withdrawn.

Despite this, the prisoners made their way out, shuffling across the litter-strewn sand. Both Darius and Trevor caught sight of Suleiman Abdi sitting in the front passenger seat of the battered Toyota Hilux pickup, his deep-set bloodshot eyes glaring at them. A rowdy group of men, all brandishing weapons, huddled on the back of a battered Mazda 3-tonne truck. Omar herded the hostages towards the Hilux, opened the tailgate and instructed them to climb in.

"Get in the back," he urged nervously. "It's a short drive down to the ocean."

Carefully, Darius seated Trevor on the tailgate, then climbed in himself, pulling him into a seated position with his back against the cab. Once everyone was settled, Omar, still carrying his weapon, jumped into the back of the truck and positioned himself to face the two prisoners. Satisfied everything was in order, he shouted a quick order in Somali, and the driver revved the engine. They lurched off down the dusty track toward the buildings and the ocean beyond.

The heat of the afternoon was brutal, with humidity nearing 100%. The short drive through the settlement of mud brick dwellings and tin shacks took no more than eight minutes. Eventually, they arrived at what seemed to be a natural harbour, with a rocky outcrop to the right and several boats moored to the left. A dilapidated and rusted canning factory stood in front of them. The driver navigated around the building, continuing toward the ocean, stopping about 30 metres away on the firm sand.

As the truck's engine stopped, Darius surveyed the landscape, feeling a surge of nervousness. He refrained from looking through the cab, instead taking in the surroundings. Omar quickly leapt from the back and swung the tailgate down.

"Come on," he urged. "Aren't you getting out? It's time to go. Hurry, hurry!"

It took a moment to help Trevor from the truck and the two prisoners were instructed to sit on the hard sand while the rest of the men disembarked from the Mazda and formed a semicircle around them. It was then that Trevor and Darius could finally gaze out at the ocean. For them, it symbolized freedom from the hell that had been Somalia and the coast of Puntland. Their salvation was due to arrive within half an hour: a saviour by boat carrying a large amount of cash to take them to medical care and freedom. The hope and desperation on their faces were evident. With a warm breeze coming off the ocean and the yellow glow of the sun setting behind them, the prisoners sat and stared wistfully out to sea.

37

CHAPTER THIRTY-SEVEN.

DESPITE THE STEADY BREEZE blowing in from the east, young Alex's face and upper body were drenched with sweat. Both of us wore heavy combat trousers, belts, and tight-fitting green T-shirts under our camera webbing. This was to visually reassure the kidnappers that we were unarmed. The fully laden RIB swung over the side of the super tanker, gradually sinking down to the ocean below. Despite the gravity of our mission, I found myself in a surprisingly light mood. It was almost as if it was a relief to be finally getting on with the job I had been hired to do. The barrage of mind-numbing preparation work was over now. Choosing not to glance at Alex any longer, I leaned over and peered down at the slowly approaching ocean. It was a deep blue colour that reminded me of lapis lazuli or Tanzanite. After a long wait, we finally detached the cables linked to the gantry crane above. Once freed, I stood behind the bridge, turned the key for the electric start and the brand-new motor roared to life instantly. *Time to go, Green*. Alex gave me a thumbs-up, which I reciprocated before pushing the throttle and feeling the raw surge of power as the agile boat leapt forward, cutting through the swells as we set off.

There was some respite from the heat, thanks to the wind on our bodies and faces as we sped westward. Glancing occasionally at the GPS screen on the console, I noticed Alex's half-smile as we navigated the waves. My course followed the green dotted line on the display precisely. Looking back, I saw the super tanker shrinking rapidly in the distance behind us. Despite our speed of 80 kilometres per hour, it was surprising how quickly it diminished. Ahead of us was only a vast expanse of ocean. With the boat comfortably on the plane, I glanced at my watch, estimating the time it would take to reach the designated GPS location for the exchange. It was imperative to arrive neither late nor early and my timing had to be precise. Adjusting our trajectory and speed, I settled in for the journey, feeling a sense of action that alleviated my fears about the looming danger.

About 25 minutes later, with only the occasional shouted exchange between Alex and me over the roar of the engine, the landmass of Somalia emerged ahead. It appeared as a cream-coloured, sandy expanse, shimmering in the late afternoon like a mirage, its edges tinted orange by the setting sun. It was an ominous yet comforting sight, given our isolation since losing sight of the super tanker.

Noticing we were running about five minutes early; I reduced the speed to adjust our arrival time. The GPS indicated we were only 4.5 kilometres from the coast, prompting me to make a brief pause once we reached the three-kilometre mark. Any deviation could potentially provoke the kidnappers, a risk I had been repeatedly warned about and was unwilling to take. Everything had to proceed as planned, meticulously on schedule. As we hit the three-kilometre mark, with the land now clearer than the blurry vision we'd initially seen, I eased back the throttle, allowing the boat to slow to a halt while the engine idled and gurgled behind us.

38

Chapter Thirty-Eight.

Suleiman Abdi's behaviour was becoming increasingly erratic as his paranoia escalated. Again and again, he glanced at the sky as if expecting an attack from some unseen aircraft. Pacing up and down on the packed sand, behind his men, he demanded answers from Omar, barking out a series of panicked questions one after another.

"Where are these devils?" he demanded. "Something is about to take place and we are about to be tricked. Something is going to go wrong, Omar. I warned you. I can feel it in my bones!"

With a look of sheer desperation on his face, Omar attempted to keep up with his frantically pacing master, desperately trying to calm and appease him.

"Everything is in order, master. Everything has been taken care of and planned meticulously," he said, a note of despair in his voice. "It is not yet time for them to arrive. We still have a good ten minutes. They are due to arrive at exactly 3:00pm."

"I don't like it! I told you before," Suleiman said "I don't like it at all. We are making a mistake here. I feel something is going to go terribly wrong!"

The conversation, fraught and full of agitation, was overheard by the men guarding the hostages nearby. This influenced them as well and all of them became nervous and jumpy upon hearing Suleiman's fears. The entire operation seemed to be in danger of falling apart at the last hurdle. In a desperate attempt to calm the situation down, Omar stood still, turned and addressed the men.

"Everyone should be calm, please!" he shouted "Do not worry, fellow warriors. Everything is under control!"

Seeing Omar trying to calm the situation, Suleiman grabbed him by his arm and pulled him away towards the canning factory, out of earshot of the bewildered hostages and the other men. Once they were a sufficient distance, he pulled Omar around with his bony hand and stared him in the eye with crazed, bloodshot eyes. The old man started hectoring him and frothy green droplets of khat-infused spittle flew from his thin lips as he did so.

"Omar," he hissed, "you can see the men are becoming agitated as well. They too fear something is about to go wrong. I will hold you personally responsible if something does."

Desperately trying to calm his master, Omar spread his hands in a conciliatory gesture.

"Master, trust me," he said, pleading. "We have been through this a hundred times. We have Faizal positioned with the RPG in the rocks on the right and a sniper near the boats on the left. We have another man behind the canning factory. Nothing can go wrong. We will easily outnumber and outgun the two men who are bringing our money. We have nothing to lose and everything to gain! The money is ours, and if anything is slightly out of order or suspicious, I will immediately call a stop to it all. Trust me, Master. Everything will be fine!"

Suleiman's jaw vibrated as he chewed furiously on the ball of khat in his mouth. The thin skin of his cheek bulged, and he spat a giant globule of greenish-brown saliva onto the sand.

"Very well," he said. "We will go ahead, but you better pray to Allah the Almighty that you are right, Omar."

But it was at that moment that the phone in Omar's pocket rang. This had an alarming effect on Suleiman, who gasped and stepped backwards. *Who is this? What is this phone call coming at this hour?* He thought. Omar pulled the device from his pocket with shaking hands and stared at the caller ID. It was the number that had been given to him by the Kaminsky people, the number of the man who was due to deliver the ransom money. Quickly, Omar glanced at the time on the screen of the phone. It was 2:55pm. *Why is this man phoning now? Is there now a problem that will prove Suleiman right?* he wondered as the sweat poured down his temples.

The name on the screen was Jason Green.

39

CHAPTER THIRTY-NINE.

"Good afternoon, Omar," I said, clutching the phone to my ear. "This is Jason Green. How are you today?"

The man on the other side of the line sounded flustered and nervous, to say the least.

"Yes, yes, I'm fine," said Omar "Why are you calling? Is there something wrong?"

"I'm glad to hear you're well, Omar," I replied. "No, nothing is wrong. I just wanted to let you know that we have arrived early and are currently sitting one kilometre from the shore. We have paused here to allow some time to pass so that we can arrive exactly on time at 3:00pm. I wanted to let you know the situation and to assure you that everything is on track. We have the ransom money on board, and everything is going smoothly. A final check I'd like to make is if the hostages are well and ready for the exchange we're about to do."

"Yes, yes, of course," said Omar spinning around and gazing at the ocean. "Of course, they are. They're on the beach with us as I speak. I had not expected this call, but of course, yes, they are on the beach. Uh, you may proceed and allow yourself to arrive on time at 3:00pm."

"Very well," I said. "I will set off in the next two minutes, so I arrive at the beach at the rendezvous point exactly at 3:00pm. Thank you, Omar, and I apologize for causing any alarm by phoning you unexpectedly."

"Thank you, yes, thank you. That is fine. Thank you, Mr Green," said Omar, frowning slightly.

I hung up, pocketed the phone and glanced at Alex, who sat below where I stood at the bridge with raised eyebrows and a half-smile on his face.

"He sounds a bit nervous," said Alex.

"Hmm," I said. "You're right, he does. Well, I suppose he's about to get the biggest payday of his life. I'm sure he's a bit nervous. Let's hope there is no problem with our people."

"Yes," said Alex, wiping the sweat from his forehead.

With the engine idling the heat and humidity descended like a wet blanket and the air was still. I glanced at my watch and spoke again.

"Okay, Alex, let's both start the live stream. In the next couple of minutes, we'll get going. Please activate the camera on your chest, and I will do the same. Just before we head off, I will confirm that everyone is hearing and seeing everything take place clearly. Are you ready?"

Alex nodded eagerly then reached down and switched his chest camera on. I did the same and immediately spoke so that the camera, which was streaming the events, would hopefully be in contact with the ship and the Kaminsky people in Krakow.

"Testing once again, this is Jason Green. Uh, does everyone read me okay? Can everyone see what's going on?"

"Affirmative," said the speaker on the console next to me. "We can hear and see you very clearly, Jason. Thank you for making contact."

This was also confirmed by Marek and Younis in Krakow, and I knew then that the mission had the green light to go ahead. It was time to go and rescue the Kaminsky people from the clutches of their kidnappers of three months. It was time to release them from the horror that they had been subjected to.

I took a deep breath, wiped the sweat from my forehead, and glanced quickly at Alex, who smiled as usual. I turned to face the console and gripped the steering wheel with my left hand.

"Right," I said before I advanced the throttle. "Let's do this."

40

Chapter Forty.

With his AK-47 rifle in his right hand, the barrel pointed down to the sand, Suleiman Abdi made his way to the left side of the group of men and hostages, Omar at his side. Once in position, some 25 metres away, he paused and stared out at the ocean. Omar, his own rifle strapped over his shoulder, lifted the pair of binoculars that hung around his neck and peered through them out at the horizon.

"I see them now," said Omar. "I can see them, master. Two men on a black boat, coming fast towards us. They are unarmed. Look, master."

Omar handed the binoculars to Suleiman, who gripped them with shaky hands and held them to his eyes. He fumbled slightly, apparently unused to using binoculars.

"Allow me to help you, Master," said Omar in a meek voice, as he carefully adjusted the binoculars for Suleiman to better see the approaching RIB.

"Yes, I see them now," Suleiman confirmed "I do not like the look of them, that is certain."

After taking the binoculars from his eyes, he handed them back to Omar, who looked up at him with a fearful, pleading expression.

"Trust me, master. Everything will be fine," Omar assured him. "Look, we do not even need binoculars to see them now. They have slowed down and are approaching us slowly and carefully. Everything is going according to plan."

As the boat grew closer, the tension among the men became apparent, and they began to clamour and jostle among themselves.

"Be calm!" shouted Omar at them. "Be calm and allow me to handle the situation."

THE CHAMELEON OF KRAKOW

Suleiman Abdi fidgeted to Omar's left, his head turning between the men and the approaching RIB. Now, it was clear to see the faces of the men who were approaching: one middle-aged, tough-looking and a younger blond man in his early 20s with brush-cut hair and an open, half-smiling expression.

But Omar's eyes settled more on the large plastic crate strapped to the bows of the RIB. This was the container holding the $3,000,000 ransom. Now within reach, the payday he had been yearning for was about to happen. The ordeal of being stuck in this dreadful settlement on the coast of Puntland, Somalia, was about to come to an end and he would be allowed to return to Mogadishu. Finally, he would escape the paranoid Suleiman Abdi and his band of roving bandits.

Cash registers began to ring in Omar's mind as he watched the boat approach the shoreline, noting that both men were completely unarmed, as per the arrangement. Both men stood with blank expressions on their faces as the boat neared.

It was then that the older man reached for the console and pulled a switch. The back of the powerful motor began to tilt as the propeller came out of the water, its momentum carrying it towards the shoreline. The boat made contact with the shore seconds later, and Omar heard the crunch of the sand under its hull.

The time had come. The exchange of prisoners for cash was about to take place, and the atmosphere was charged with electricity.

41

Chapter Forty-One.

As the boat drew closer to the shore, my gaze immediately sought out the faces of the hostages I had memorized so well. Soon enough, I spotted them sitting on the sand in front of a group of maybe ten or twelve armed men. The men wore dirty robes and seemed armed to the teeth, looking slightly agitated and jumpy, while the hostages looked frail, resigned and drawn. Next, I forced my attention away from them to search for the other two characters I had committed to memory. I found Suleiman Abdi and Omar standing some distance to the right, perhaps twenty metres away. I flicked the trim to lift the motor and behind me, the whirring of the propeller lifting from the water signalled our approach towards the sand. In that split second, my brain registered that Suleiman Abdi, the older of the men on the right, appeared jumpy and twitchy, but I quickly dismissed the thought. *Just do the job, Green.* The plan had been rehearsed hundreds of times, and my foremost priority was the well-being and safety of the hostages.

Soon enough, the boat hit the shore and I heard the sand crunch under the rigid hull as we came to a halt. The afternoon sun was fierce and sweat poured from every pore of my body. I stumbled forward slightly as the motor was cut and suddenly, all was silent. It was a stark contrast to the travel and noise of the past days. It felt as if a giant wet blanket had descended upon me, my forearm was glistening with sweat as I turned the ignition key off. For a few seconds that felt like an eternity, I stood there, dead still, scanning the situation before me. My eyes eventually fell on the clearly ill figure of Trevor Nichol, but I knew my immediate contact needed to be Omar. Forcing a smile, I turned my head and greeted him.

"Good afternoon, Omar. It's great to finally meet you."

THE CHAMELEON OF KRAKOW

I waited for what felt like an age for his reply. Thankfully, he spoke within a few seconds,

"Yes, Mr. Green, it is I, Omar. It's very great to see you and we hope that our business can be concluded quickly so everyone can be on their way."

"That is the plan," I called out. "With your permission, I will now step to the front of the boat with my colleague, and we will unshackle the crate containing the money and carry it onto the beach, as per our arrangement."

There was a pause as Omar consulted Suleiman Abdi in a voice I couldn't hear. Once again, I had the strange feeling that Suleiman was agitated, but I forced the paranoid thought from my mind. There appeared to be some disagreement or frustration and I wondered if I had been right to suspect there was a problem. So much preparation had gone into this moment; it seemed odd that something could go wrong at such a late stage. But thankfully, Omar turned again, faced me and called out,

"Yes, that is fine. You may proceed to unshackle the crate and bring it onto the sand in front of us. Please make no sudden movements and do everything slowly and smoothly. We don't want to alarm anyone here."

"Thank you, Omar," I said. "I assure you, there will be no issues. We are here to do a transaction, that is all. We will now go and unshackle the crate."

After another pause, Omar shouted,

"Yes, please go ahead."

I turned to look at Alex and nodded at him. The procedure, which had been rehearsed in my mind thousands of times and drummed into my memory, was about to begin. Alex knew exactly what needed to be done and we both moved forward, holding our arms out at our sides to show we were unarmed. This gesture was meant to reassure the kidnappers. In my earpiece, there was only silence, and I was aware that the captain aboard the super tanker and the viewers in Krakow were watching and listening to our every move. I imagined they would be watching with bated breath.

Stepping forward, Alex and I released the latches on the ratchets that held the plastic crate of money down. With a nod from myself, Alex bent over and grabbed the handle on the left side of the crate while I did the same on the other. The 30kg came up easily enough and both of us glanced towards Omar once we had lifted it before I called once again.

"We have lifted the case, Omar. We will now bring it over and place it on the sand."

After a pause for Omar to consult Suleiman, he called out,

"Yes, please go ahead. Bring it up onto the sand and place it down."

"Very well," I replied. "We will do that right away."

I nodded at Alex, and we eased forward, stepping over the inflatable side of the RIB into the shallow, bath-warm water. The appalling humidity and the fierce afternoon sun were palpable as the wet sand squeaked underfoot. The tension was incredible as we worked, the only sound was the sloshing of water around my ankles.

But as we transitioned from the wet sand to the dry, a murmur of discontent among the men behind the seated hostages became apparent. Glancing to the right at the figures of Omar and Suleiman, I saw Suleiman increasingly agitated, speaking frantically to Omar, who seemed to be in a panic. What the fuck is going on here? I thought. Something's up, something's not right, that's for sure. But it was too late, and we were committed. Alex and I continued walking up the beach for another 10 metres before placing the crate down and then standing bolt upright. By then, the men behind the seated hostages were stirring and moving erratically. The atmosphere had shifted from one of relative calm to one of panic and impending doom.

"Is everything all right, Omar?" I called out loudly.

But Omar was already in frantic conversation with Suleiman, who appeared paranoid, glancing from left to right and up to the sky as if expecting some attack. Standing there, I could only feel my heart sinking as the situation began to spiral out of control. Everything began unfolding in slow motion. The men behind the seated hostages raised a cacophony of shouts and jeers, darting erratically from left to right. My gaze, however, was fixed on the hostages. Their safety was my primary concern.

I watched their expressions shift to one of resignation, a heavy sense of pity welling up inside me. I knew they understood there was no escape that day.

Yet, at the very next moment, my attention snapped back to the immediate crisis. My eyes shifted right, focusing on Omar. With his arms outstretched, he seemed to be frantically pleading with Suleiman Abdi. The elder, however, appeared almost overcome with panic, glancing about as if pursued by phantoms. The jeers and hoots from the others only heightened his distress.

"What's happening here, Omar?" I shouted, trying to cut through the chaos. "There's no need for panic!"

Instinctively, I raised my hands, noticing from the corner of my eye that Alex had done the same. This gesture was meant to drum in the fact we were unarmed, standing vulnerably on the sand.

"Omar!" I shouted through gritted teeth. "Calm your men down. This isn't the time to lose it. We've come too far!"

But it was too late. The translator was too preoccupied with appealing to his superior to heed my calls. It was then that Suleiman's eyes locked on to mine, his gaze searing. As he slowly raised his right arm, clutching an AK47, I braced myself for the worst. But rather than aiming at us, he lifted the weapon skyward. That was the moment chaos erupted.

Bullets began to pepper the sand around us, their origin hidden within the dilapidated factory and the rocks and boats flanking us. Frozen in place, I watched as young Alex's courage faltered, his earlier resolve shattered by the grim realization of our predicament.

"Alex, stay with me!" I yelled over the gunfire, but he was already sprinting towards the boat, his actions sparking further panic among the men and the unseen assailants. As the situation descended into utter chaos, I dived to the left, landing on my stomach in the sand. I lost all concern for the hostages, focusing solely on survival. I looked back and watched Alex leap towards the RIB, seeking cover, but my attention was soon drawn to a figure emerging from behind the rocks. The man was tall and seemed to have a distorted sneer on his face. But it was then that I saw him raise the rocket-propelled grenade launcher. With wide, crazed eyes, he brought up the steel tube and deftly placed it on his right shoulder, his aim behind me on the beached RIB. *No, no, please God no!* But it was too late. In excruciating slow motion, I watched him fire the missile. Its trajectory was precise as it streaked across the beach leaving a trail of smoke and striking the RIB's bridge console directly. The explosion was immediate and devastating and it sent a blast of sand and spray and fire that singed the hair on my arm. Alex was obliterated and the RIB was reduced to a fiery wreck, leaving nothing but a towering mushroom cloud of smoke and flames. Miraculously shielded by the plastic crate, I was spared the full brunt of the blast. Now unarmed and under attack, I could do nothing but lie there, watching the remnants of the boat as a mob descended upon me. They unleashed a brutal onslaught, their kicks and punches relentless. What had begun as a simple transaction had spiralled into a hideous orgy of violence and destruction—a screaming nightmare of blood, smoke and fire that left me on the brink of unconsciousness.

42

Chapter Forty-Two.

After the tumult and shocking scenes broadcast on the screens, the control room at Kaminski Logistica in Poland descended into silence. Younis Bader leaned back in his seat, his gaze falling to the floor, his eyes brimming with unshed tears. Marek Kaminski sat motionless, staring at the now-blank screens, his jaw muscles twitching uncontrollably, a vacant expression on his youthful, handsome face. Barry Matthews remained fixated on the screens, his fingers drumming on the tabletop in a rhythmic echo of the room's tense silence. The atmosphere crackled with a palpable tension, but the prevailing mood was one of unmistakable disappointment and shock.

After a long, heavy pause, Marek Kaminski pushed his chair back, stood up and with robotic precision, turned to exit the conference room that had served as their command centre for the past three months. He walked slowly down the corridor to his office, pushing the door open to find his wife, Andrea, who had been anxiously awaiting good news under his instructions. Her face which had been alight with anticipation, fell at the sight of Marek's stone-cold demeanour. A wave of concern washed over her, and she instinctively brought her hand to her chest. Marek, ignoring his wife's worried glance, walked past her to his desk. Once there, he circled the large desk and sat down, his jaw still clenched, eyes distant behind his rimless glasses. He stared out through the large windows at the forest beyond, lost in thought or perhaps in another world entirely. Sensing the gravity of the situation, Andrea rose and approached him, attempting to offer some comfort.

"Marek, what happened? My love, please, tell me."

Marek remained unresponsive. It was only when she moved to physically comfort him that he suddenly raised his hand in a stopping gesture, still not meeting her gaze.

"Get out," he bellowed, a command so uncharacteristic that it rooted her to the spot in shock.

Marek had never raised his voice to his wife before and this sudden outburst was utterly foreign. Frozen, she stared at her husband, now a stranger in this moment of raw emotion, his hand still raised in forbiddance. Marek yelled again, this time his voice was louder, and his raised hand shook with rage.

"Get out! Get out!!" his voice echoing in the spacious office.

Tears welled up in Andrea's eyes as she trembled, the realization of her husband's distress and her own shock mingling. With a gasp of horror, she turned, grabbed her handbag from the couch and cast one last look at Marek. He remained a stoic figure with his gaze fixed outside, unseeing. With her heart breaking, Andrea ran to the door, pulled it open and left the office, leaving behind a silence that spoke volumes about the day's harrowing events. Younis only lifted his tear-streaked eyes at the sight of Marek's wife fleeing down the corridor, her distress evident through the heavy glass partition that separated him from the corridor. With the bank of screens now dark, a heavy silence enveloped the communications room, only to be broken thirty seconds later by Captain Butterfield's voice crackling through the speakers.

"Marek, are you there?" the captain's voice conveyed urgency and concern, a stark contrast to the stunned silence that had just been prevailing.

"Marek, can you hear me? This is Captain Butterfield," he repeated, his message cutting through the quiet.

Barry Matthews responded with a slight croak in his voice,

"Butterfield, this is Matthews. I'm sorry, Marek has left the room."

There was a brief pause before Captain Butterfield spoke again. Matthews quickly tapped at the keyboard, and suddenly, the captain's drawn and pale face appeared on the main screen, mirroring the gravity of the situation they had all witnessed on the live stream.

"There you are," said Butterfield, the relief evident in his voice as the webcams came back to life.

"Well," said Mathews clearing his throat, "Let's acknowledge the reality. I'll need to review the recordings to understand what went wrong. But right now, our priority is to address our current predicament. At the moment it appears we've lost one man, the medic who ran back to the shoreline. The fate of Green and the hostages remains uncertain. The live stream ended after the explosion, and as we saw, chaos ensued. I suggest we wait half an hour, then try to contact Omar again. Whatever happened on that beach, the kidnappers now have the money, and they still hold our people, including Green. I'm sorry, Captain. This has indeed turned into a nightmare, but our only course is to try to extricate our people from this disaster. However, the situation is undoubtedly dire. As I mentioned, let's give it half an hour to let things settle, then we'll hold another conference call with Omar and try to determine our next move."

Barry Matthews glanced at Younis, who closed his eyes, shook his head and nodded in agreement, signalling that proceeding as suggested was the only viable option.

"Very well," Captain Butterfield said, determination in his tone. "I'll be here on standby, ready to watch and listen when we make the call. God help us, gentlemen. God help our people."

43

Chapter Forty-Three.

Amid the chaos, the heat and the violence, I found myself the object of a brutal assault. Despite my efforts to shield my head and face, I was dimly aware of a barrage of kicks, punches and rifle butts raining down on me from every direction. The surreal horror of my predicament was somewhat dulled by a bizarre detachment as if I were observing the ordeal from a distance. Stunned by the sudden ferocity and chaos of the explosions, screams and gunfire, it felt as though I was watching the events unfold from above, my body numbed by the sheer magnitude of the horror. Mercifully, the physical beating started to wane, giving way to hands that frantically stripped me of my webbing, tore the GoPro from its mount, and rifled through my pockets. The shouts in the guttural Somali dialect filled the air as I was jostled about, the setting sun blinded me, and the day's intense heat exacerbated my suffering.

Dazed, confused, and in shock, I was vaguely aware of being hoisted by my arms and ankles, struggling to maintain consciousness and desperate to catch a glimpse of the hostages, but to no avail. Reality ebbed and flowed, and I had an overwhelming thirst and a body wracked with pain. Abruptly, I found myself dumped onto a scorching metal floor, hands pinning me down, rendering me immobile. I lay there, the metal's searing heat paradoxically helping me cling to reality, attempting to grasp my surroundings, but it was a futile effort. The beating had been merciless, pushing me to the limits of my endurance. The events that had unfolded were too horrific to fully comprehend. The image of young Alex obliterated in the RIB, which was meant to be our salvation, haunted me. The root cause of the disastrous exchange eluded me, but I knew my circumstances were dire and likely to worsen. Gradually, I became aware of a vibration beneath the metal floor and realized I had been thrown into the back of a pickup truck.

Amid the ongoing shouts and confusion, I tried to focus on the engine's revving. Every so often, I would open my eyes only to see a blur of robes, black limbs, blue sky and the scrubby wasteland as the pickup jolted over rough terrain. Our destination was unknown to me, but the jarring motion suggested we were headed inland. As the darkness began to encroach, there was a perverse comfort in succumbing to unconsciousness, almost a relief to drift away from the relentless nightmare.

The next sensation that gripped me was the cacophony of voices, all of them tense, angry, shouting in both Somali and English. In my confusion, their words melded into an indistinguishable racket. Once again, hands gripped me under my arms and around my ankles, hoisting me up and carrying me away at speed. I attempted to open my eyes, but the glaring sun reduced my vision to a mere blur of images. People running, shouting and screaming. Chaos enveloped everything as I drifted in and out of consciousness.

Soon after I felt myself being thrown onto a hard, concrete surface. Inside this new enclosure, the humidity was oppressive and the voices around me grew louder, though now, more were speaking English. Then came the resounding slam of a metal door, followed by the distinct sound of padlocks securing it. Thankfully, this seemed to mark the end of the earlier tumult. A semblance of quiet ensued, albeit a deeply uncomfortable one due to the hard surface beneath me and the stifling humidity.

As my breathing gradually steadied, I lay there, immobilized, eyes closed, forcing myself to calm down. I needed to process the nightmare unfolding of events that had led to such a devastating loss of life.

44

Chapter Forty-Four.

Approximately twenty minutes later, Marek re-entered the control room at the company headquarters in Krakow. A heavy silence filled the room as Younis and Matthews watched him intently. Marek's expression was one of grim resignation and he moved with his characteristic, almost mechanical stride. Pulling out a chair, he sat down and intertwined his fingers, resting his forearms on the gleaming surface of the expensive desk. He acknowledged Matthews and Younis with a nod, appreciating their presence before he cleared his throat to speak.

"Barry, would you mind contacting Captain Butterfield for us? I believe it's time we held a meeting to discuss our current predicament. We need to align our thoughts on how to proceed."

Matthews cleared his throat, leaned forward and began to operate the keyboard in front of him, establishing a connection with the captain of the super tanker anchored off the coast of Somalia.

"Yes, that's the prudent step. We mustn't let our emotions cloud our judgment. The earlier events were regrettable, but we must stay focused on the path ahead. We need confirmation on the statuses of Green and the hostages. And though it's distressing to consider, we must also confront the possibility that the kidnappers have betrayed us, taking the ransom and harming the hostages." He said.

Younis, visibly tense and emotional, leaned in.

"That's inconceivable," he said.

"It's inconceivable, yet entirely within the realm of possibility," Marek replied, his tone now firm.

After a brief pause, the screen flickered to life, revealing Captain Butterfield.

"I'm at a loss for words, gentlemen. We were close, yet it feels like we've achieved nothing. The crew are heartbroken."

"I understand," Matthews responded, "but we must look ahead. Our immediate priority is to conference call Omar to understand the situation better. We complied fully with their demands, but something went awry. We need to ascertain the health and status of our people. Let's proceed calmly and without emotion. Once we reach Omar, who may be agitated, I ask that you allow me to lead the conversation. Is that clear?"

Murmurs of agreement filled the room and resonated from the large screen, signalling consensus from everyone.

"Right," Matthews concluded, "Let's get on with it."

45

CHAPTER FORTY-FIVE.

Completely disregarding the smouldering wreckage of the RIB and the scattered remains along the beach, the group of men jeered and danced around the heavy plastic crate, their shouts filled with glee. This scene mirrored the chaos of the preceding moments when the RPG had obliterated the boat and claimed the life of one of the hostage rescue team. It seemed this was of no concern at all. Seeking to quell the frenzy, Suleiman Abdi fired three shots into the air. The men, momentarily stunned, turned to see the commanding presence of the tall, elderly man approaching. Behind him, in contrast, Omar appeared, his demeanour inept and fraught with worry.

"Step back!" Suleiman shouted, his voice cutting through the noise.

The men, recognizing their leader's authority, instantly fell silent and backed away from the crate. Reaching it, Suleiman eyed it, clearly suspicious of potential traps. Turning to Omar, he barked out an order,

"Open this box now. I'll be watching."

Omar, visibly distressed, frantically agreed. Suleiman stepped back, maintaining a safe distance as Omar worked the latches of the crate. With the final latch undone, Omar looked to Suleiman for approval before lifting the lid. The anticipation of a trap loomed, but the lid opened without incident, revealing its contents. Upon seeing the contents, Omar's eyes widened in shock. Suleiman, after a brief pause, approached to inspect the crate himself. Inside, packaged into neat bricks, was the $3,000,000 ransom money promised by Kaminski Logistica. The absence of traps or deceit was clear, and the money lay there for all to see. Still cautious, Suleiman instructed Omar to secure the crate once more. He then directed the men to load it onto one of the vehicles and transport it to the armoury for further inspection. The men, elated by the sight of their long-awaited payment, hoisted the crate onto the back of a truck and set off towards the small, dusty settlement. Once they arrived, they approached a low brick building, distinct in its solidity with a heavy steel roof and door but no windows at all. As the sun set over Puntland's vast landscape, Suleiman entered the armoury, flicking on a light powered by a solar array.

Settling on an ammunition box, Suleiman watched as Omar, seemingly overwhelmed yet diligent, began to carefully unload the money. Each brick of $100,000 was methodically placed on the concrete floor under Suleiman's watchful eye.

46

CHAPTER FORTY-SIX.

"Wake up, wake up," said the voice in my mind.

Confusion swirled around me. The voice was familiar and for a few moments, I had no idea where I was. Then, I noticed someone's knee next to my face. A man was kneeling beside me, his voice coaxing me again,

"Wake up, wake up. Here, drink some water..."

A trickle of brackish liquid entered my mouth as my head was gently tilted to one side by the man. The sensation aroused me from my unconscious state. I forced my eyes open, only to find my left eye swollen shut from the beating I had received. Still, my right eye was functional. I blinked a few times in the darkness, allowing my vision to adjust to the gloom. For a moment, I was lost, not knowing where I was.

His face hovered above me, appearing blurred. The water he fed me was a lifesaver, gradually bringing my senses back. I cleared my throat after swallowing some more of the brackish water and managed to croak,

"Where am I?"

"You are the guest of Suleiman Abdi, just as we have been for the past three months," he explained. "We watched you arrive on the boat to come and rescue us and then we saw everything go wrong. We're very sorry, but the young man you arrived with is dead."

Suddenly, it all came back to me. As my brain cleared, I forced myself up onto my right elbow. The man who had given me the water was Darius Ayman. One of the hostages.

"Yes, I remember now," I said. "There was a rocket. I watched it get fired and I watched it hit the boat. My young friend Alex, are you sure he's dead?"

"I'm afraid so," said another man's voice.

I turned my head to see the skinny figure of Trevor Nichol sitting in the corner, his face drawn, bleak and dejected.

"We watched it happen," he added quietly.

Feeling some strength return, I attempted to lift my body into a sitting position. Although my head spun briefly, I managed it, despite my body aching all over. My gaze shifted from Trevor back to Darius.

"We are all in a dire situation," said Darius bleakly.

"I know," I said, my voice grim. "Everything had been meticulously planned, but something went horribly wrong."

"It was that lunatic, Suleiman," said Darius. "He's mad, paranoid and sees threats everywhere."

He described how the chaos erupted when the man with the rocket launcher destroyed the boat, killing Alex.

"I don't think we're ever going to get out of here," he concluded.

"Well," I said, my brain continuing to clear, "We'll see about that..."

I looked up to the small window, sealed off with heavy steel bars, the only source of light in the cell. It was late afternoon outside. Noticing my watch was missing, stripped along with everything else I had been wearing except for my vest and combat trousers.

"What time is it?" I asked.

"About 5:00 in the afternoon," Darius replied. "We can tell by the position of the sun and the shadows outside the window."

I nodded, absorbing the information. Darius added that this time, Sulieman had stationed a guard outside named Faizal, a hated figure known for taunting them and being trigger-happy and violent.

"He's the one who fired the rocket that killed your friend." He said grimly.

With a renewed sense of determination, I forced myself to stand, carefully shuffling over to the window to assess our surroundings. Despite the pain and aches from the savage beating, no bones felt broken. Outside, I spotted Faizal, the guard, sitting nearby on a white plastic chair, smoking a cigarette. I immediately recognised the man. His face was twisted, and it appeared that he had been born with a cleft palate. His mouth was vertically elongated, and his yellowed teeth stuck out at wild angles. Despite the fading light, I watched the man as he scrolled on his phone, seemingly pleased with himself for the murder he had committed earlier. You're going to pay dearly for what you did, my friend.

Returning to my cellmates, I sat down once again and spoke,

"Don't worry," I said, "We *will* get out of here."

47

Chapter Forty-Seven.

"Good afternoon, Omar," Barry Matthews said, his voice calm but his face red with rage.

"Hello, Barry," replied Omar, his voice sounding very distraught.

At the same time, he seemed to be trying to maintain his composure, but there was no doubt he was more than a little flustered.

"Thank you for taking our call," said Matthews. "What happened? What went wrong this afternoon?"

There was a pause on the line and the tension in the boardroom was palpable. All that could be heard was the sound of the wind and slight panting from Omar.

"I would not like to comment on the events of this afternoon at this time," said Omar. "I will be able to give you a fuller answer tomorrow when we have another conference call."

"But you can confirm that our people are alive?" Matthews asked.

"As I said, I will not deny or confirm anything at this time," Omar replied.

"Everything was arranged," said Matthews, frustration finally boiling over in his voice. "We have been working on this deal for months now and you can understand that we are extremely disappointed and concerned about our people. Can you at least confirm that you have the money and that our people are alive?"

"Listen to me!" shouted Omar, clearly flustered. "I told you before, I cannot confirm or deny anything. I am sorry that things did not work out as planned, believe me, I am as sorry as everyone else. But this will have to be cleared up tomorrow. I am under instructions from Suleiman not to talk to you. Please, let us continue this conversation tomorrow. Am I understood?"

There was a pause in the control room as Matthews, Marek and Younis faced each other, their frustration at breaking point.

"Very well, Omar," said Matthews in a controlled voice. "We will message you tomorrow and set up a time for yet another conference call. Thank you, and goodbye."

"What the fuck?" Marek burst out. "What the fuck are these people doing? Do they take us for complete idiots?"

"No," Matthews replied, his voice steady. "Clearly, something went badly wrong. What exactly, we don't know, and we will not know until we hear from them tomorrow."

"What about Jason and the medic? What about our people?" Marek shouted, his clenched fist slamming into the desk.

"There's nothing we can do. I know how helpless you feel," Matthews admitted, doing his best to return the room to calm.

At that moment, Younis brought his left hand up to his head and wiped his face. Although the control room was air-conditioned, he was sweating visibly.

"That is the position we are in, gentlemen," Matthews summed up, "We cannot change this. We must go with what Omar has told us. As to whether Green, the medic, or indeed any of our people are alive, I have no idea. We must hope and pray that they are. These people have the ransom money now and we must hope that, in some vestige of their minds, of their humanity, they will follow through and set our people free. We know that there was an explosion. We know nothing more than that. In my mind, as far as my experience goes with Somalians, I am thinking that they will be freed and I'm praying that they will be freed. Perhaps they will be left somewhere on the coast and a message sent for us to collect them. But until tomorrow, I'm afraid we must all accept that there is nothing we can do. I'm truly, truly sorry, gentlemen, but I think we all should go home and rest. I know that you are all extremely disappointed, and I know that the families of our men will be devastated. But we *have to wait until tomorrow.*"

CHAPTER FORTY-EIGHT.

THE COUNTING PROCESS TOOK four hours. It was well after 8:00pm when Omar and Suleiman emerged from the armoury, their faces alight with triumph. By then, the men waiting outside had grown jumpy and impatient. However, the news that they had indeed received the full ransom of $3,000,000 sent them into a wild frenzy of celebration. They fired their weapons into the night sky, leapt around and whooped and hollered with glee.

Eventually, Suleiman Abdi calmed the men and instructed two of them to carry the plastic crate of money out of the armoury and take it to his residence. In a triumphant speech, Suleiman explained that there would be a substantial payday the following morning, where each member of their band would receive their share for their role in the kidnapping and the successful receipt of the ransom money. No mention was made of the ill-fated hostage rescue attempt, which was the last thing on the men's minds. Once the crate was safely placed in Suleiman Abdi's residence, the men were instructed to go off and celebrate as they saw fit.

Needing no further encouragement, they quickly dispersed, their mood still buoyant, to engage in drinking, listening to music and firing their weapons as was their custom. The amount of khat chewed that night was substantial. But it was Omar who remained at Suleiman's residence after the men had gone. There was to be a conversation he had been dreading, but one he knew he needed to have.

"Master," said Omar, "I know everyone is happy and celebrating, but there are some questions I need to ask. May I?"

Suleiman, taking his usual seat against the thick mud-brick wall, slowly poured a cup of steaming green tea. He considered Omar's question, delicately lifting the cup by its thin handle and bringing it to his mouth. A deep slurping sound filled the room. Omar watched, sweat running down his temples. Finally, Suleiman placed the cup back on the tray in front of him and slowly lifted his eyes.

"Yes, you may go ahead. What would you like to know?"

"Master," Omar said, "You know our arrangement with our principal in Poland. After the debacle on the beach and the death of the young man from the hostage extraction team, there will be questions and there will be anger, I am certain. What am I to say?"

Suleiman Abdi took a deep breath, his deeply sunken eyes glowing with greed, and his face exuding a sense of accomplishment.

"Omar," he said slowly and thoughtfully, "There is a great debt owed to us by those who have destroyed our fishing waters. The $3,000,000 we have received today is only a fraction of what should be ours. Yes, I expect some contention from our principal in Poland, but remember, it is I who controls this situation. Regardless, we have the money now so that should suffice. *I* will decide the fate of the hostages, and I am in no rush to do so. The prisoners remain in the cell where they have been for the past three months, now joined by the surviving member of the hostage rescue team. We are in control. So, when you receive your call from Poland this evening, convey this sentiment. Make it understood that it is I, Suleiman Abdi, who will decide their fate. I have decided to sleep on it. It has been a great hardship getting to this point, and finally getting this money, so I need to rest before making any decisions on the way forward. That is the message, Omar. Suleiman Abdi will update them tomorrow. Nothing will be said before then. Am I clear?"

Omar, unable to hold Suleiman's gaze, briefly looked away before replying,

"Of course, master. Your wisdom, as usual, is supreme. For now, the men are celebrating, as you know. They are very happy. I shall go and rest and wait for the telephone call from Poland. I will visit you again tomorrow. I bid you a good night, my master."

With that, Suleiman Abdi closed his eyes and nodded slowly. He reached forward with his bony, jet-black hand and lifted the cup of green tea slowly to his thin lips. Omar stood up, his face still shiny with sweat, turned around and made his way to the door.

49

Chapter Forty-Nine.

The night was quiet, save for the raucous noise emanating from the celebration in the nearby township. It was evident the men were overjoyed at having secured their money and were seemingly indifferent to the life taken in the process. Inside the cell, the atmosphere was starkly different. Sombre and silent, with Trevor Nichol's condition noticeably deteriorating.

Though my own injuries were superficial, causing aches throughout my body, my mind remained clear. The enveloping darkness only served to underscore the dire conditions we were subjected to, the cell's oppressive heat and humidity, the scant and brackish water supply and the barely edible food rations that arrived around 7:00pm slid through a small flap at the bottom of the heavy steel door. The meal—a pile of dried flatbread and a bowl of gruel that smelled foul—did little to improve our spirits. It was no surprise the hostages were in such poor health, with Trevor Nichol particularly affected, curled up in a corner in considerable distress.

After we had eaten and Darius had attempted in vain to coax Trevor into doing the same, we gathered at the far end of the cell to share my plan. Before speaking, I glanced out of the window to ensure the oddly complacent guard, preoccupied with his phone on a flimsy plastic chair, remained unaware of our conversation.

"How long will he be out there?" I inquired.

"We have no idea," Darius responded. "This is the first time they've posted a guard. Usually, the place is unattended until the boy shows up."

"And when does he come?" I pressed on.

"Usually around 10:00pm," Darius added. "He's the one who brings us water and food. Without him, we'd be in dire straits."

"Does he speak English?" I whispered.

"No, but Darius communicates with him in basic Arabic," he replied.

With the presence of the guard, I had to adjust our plan accordingly.

"Given there's a guard tonight, it's unlikely the boy will come. We'll wait until much later to make our move."

"There's no way out," Darius said quietly, his expression one of defeat.

"There's always a way," I said.

Standing in the moonlight, I removed my belt to reveal a hidden weapon. To the untrained eye, it appeared to be a regular belt, but it housed a 2-and-a-half-inch stainless steel dagger, the buckle serving as the handle. The blade was quickly deployed, catching the moonlight and drawing widened eyes from Darius as I gripped it firmly.

The buckle knife had been ingeniously concealed within the leather of the belt near the clasp. Shaped like an arrowhead, the double-sided blade was razor sharp with a flat steel shaft behind the blade that opened into a 'T' shape. It was this 'T' section of the flat handle that was designed to be held between the middle and ring fingers with the shaft of the blade protruding between the knuckles. I secured my belt once more, stole another glance at the guard through the window, and then sat down with Darius.

"What's your plan?" Darius whispered.

"I'll wait until the guard is less vigilant," I said quietly "Judging by the moon, I can estimate it'll be around midnight. That's when I'll make my move."

"What will you do?"

"We need to lure him inside. We must create a reason for him to enter," I said.

"And then?" he asked.

"The guard must be neutralized before we have any chance of getting away. Once he's incapacitated, we need to get past the township and down to the harbour. There, we must secure fuel for a boat and set course for the Kaminski ship which is 100 kilometres offshore. All the while we must make sure Suleiman and his men have no idea what's going on. It will be tricky, but I think we can pull it off."

Darius's face, despite the despair brought on by the failed rescue attempt, lit up with a flicker of hope.

"Okay," said Darius, his voice a mixture of resolve and desperation. "It sounds like a plan. If we don't act, Trevor won't last much longer."

"I know," I said, feeling the weight of our predicament. "We leave tonight. Trust me..."

50

Chapter Fifty.

Omar was a man sick with worry. For two hours, he sat in the stinking hot confines of his metal shack, occasionally lying down, occasionally pacing across the hard-packed dirt floor. All the while, he glanced at his cell phone, awaiting the call that he knew would come. The pressure he was under was immense and the fact that Suleiman Abdi had destroyed their plan so thoroughly was beyond belief to him. He knew that there would be trouble and a price to pay. What had happened was far beyond the plan and now, there would be fallout to deal with. Again and again, in his mind, he cursed the paranoia and madness of Suleiman. *What had he thought was going to happen? Had he been seeing shadows or ghosts as usual?* The torment of the last three months, working with the insane warlord, had taken its toll on Omar. If he had had his way, he would have killed Suleiman, stolen the ransom money and moved on. But the coast of Somalia was a dangerous place, and this was no time to be questioning the authority of the warlord.

The music, cheering and howling of the men nearby, as they celebrated in the makeshift shebeen, was deafening. The heat and humidity of the night were appalling, causing him to sweat profusely from every pore in his body. Even the grimy mattress on which he lay down occasionally was damp with his own sweat and stank of body odour. At one stage during the night, he carried his phone out along with a bucket of seawater and doused himself with the water in an effort to cool down. But this had no effect, such was the humidity and heat of the night. It was at around 10:30pm that the call came. At the time, Omar had been lying on his filthy mattress. Sitting up quickly, he snatched the device and stared at the screen. As usual, the country code showed the call was coming from Poland.

"Hello," he answered nervously.

"What the fuck happened, Omar? What sort of hell have you allowed to happen?"

"It was not I," said Omar out loud, exasperated. "I had nothing to do with it, boss. It was Suleiman, all along. The man is paranoid. He sees ghosts everywhere. Everything was set up so well and then he destroyed it. *He* gave the signal for the rescue boat to be destroyed."

"How on earth could you have allowed this to happen, you idiot?" said the voice on the phone.

Omar's voice broke in frustration. Here he was, between a rock and a hard place, literally, with his principal in Poland and his master, the strange and paranoid madman Suleiman Abdi, on the other.

"Like I said, it was beyond my control. Suleiman is a madman. All I wanted was for the transaction to go ahead as planned. It was he who caused the explosion and the attack on the boat. It was he who made this problem. We set up and arranged this whole thing and included Suleiman to act as a front. A willing partner in what would be a lucrative, ongoing business. I have done my part for three months, living in this hell, trying to organize this deal and everything is destroyed in one afternoon by Suleiman."

"We still have the money," said the voice on the phone.

"Yes, we have the money," said Omar. "But we still have the problem of the prisoners and now, I don't know what to do. Perhaps Suleiman will kill them, I have no idea."

"Well, that will be something which we will look at as collateral damage," said the voice. "I know it was not supposed to go this way, but there is little we can do. But I am deeply concerned about Suleiman. It is clear we can no longer trust him going forward. It is all too apparent that the man is no longer trustworthy or sane. In fact, his paranoia has reached such alarming levels that I don't think we can deal with him anymore. Omar, I think our next move will be to take our portion of the money and eliminate Suleiman."

There was a long pause, and Omar closed his eyes in fear and trepidation as he wiped sweat from his forehead.

"Dear God," said Omar. "No, this gets more and more complicated and here I am, trapped in the middle."

"It is three million U.S. dollars, Omar. A small sacrifice must be made for our futures here. Do you not think so? Have you not worked hard enough?"

"Yes, yes, I have," said Omar. "Yes, we all have. But what to do?"

"Well," said the voice, "I think our next move must wait until tomorrow. Suleiman has sent a very clear message that he will sleep on the current situation and make his decision.

The way forward will be set out by him and only him, tomorrow. Let him continue to think he is in control. Once we have heard what his plan is, then we can make our own. If he is willing to release the prisoners, then we will go with it. If he decides to kill them, then there is nothing we can do about that. But for the moment, there is great disappointment."

"I know," said Omar. "I know."

"So be it," said the voice. "We will wait until tomorrow and I will call you then. Goodbye, Omar."

"Goodbye, boss," said Omar, as he hung up.

Omar placed the phone on the makeshift bedside table and hung his head low in his hands in a deep state of worry and fear.

51

CHAPTER FIFTY-ONE.

For the next two hours, I rigorously went over my plan of action. Despite having committed the encampment's layout to memory from the satellite photos, the initial hurdle was of course eliminating the strange-looking guard stationed outside our cell. The man they called Faizal, the man who had pulled the trigger that had killed young Alex. The real challenge lay in getting the hostages to the shoreline. Particularly Trevor Nichol, whose illness meant he'd need to be carried. This entailed navigating through or near the bandits' camp. Given the cover of night and the distant sounds of their raucous celebrations, I believed it was feasible. But the task was daunting because of Trevor's condition, which would slow our progress. Nevertheless, Darius, despite his own trials, seemed resilient enough to assist.

Over and over, I visualized the camp's layout, confident in my knowledge of Suleiman Abdi's residence and the armoury's location. However, the presence of lookouts or guards was an uncertainty. *They're too busy celebrating, Green.* We would be relying on moonlight to traverse the rugged terrain and I could only hope it would work in our favour. The next challenge would be securing a boat capable of taking us 100 kilometres out to sea to rendezvous with the Kaminski vessel. I knew there were several boats moored there but fuel availability and efficiency remained questions.

Even if we managed to reach the shore, commandeered a seaworthy boat, and motored 100 kilometres offshore, there was no guarantee the tanker's crew would recognize us and not mistake us for Somali pirates. Stranded on the Somali coast with no means to communicate with the Kaminski ship, we were completely isolated. The myriad of uncertainties weighed heavily on me as I sat in the oppressive humidity of the dark cell watching the hostages' moonlit faces with their expressions of hope looking to me for salvation. The senseless murder of young Alex fuelled my shock and anger and hardened my resolve to show no mercy should we encounter resistance. Occasionally, I would stand up to watch the guard outside. Once, he briefly disappeared, only to return with water and crisps, contentedly scrolling through his phone, comfortable and completely oblivious to our potential escape plans. Two hours later, I called Darius over to share my strategy.

"Listen," I whispered, "I'm going to lure the guard inside by causing a bit of a disturbance. Nothing hectic, just some quiet sounds to get his interest. Once he steps in, I'll handle the rest. If we create a loud commotion, he'll be angry and on the offensive, but if I quietly tamper with the cell door's hinges, it'll pique his curiosity and fool him into thinking he has the upper hand. But I need your help, Darius. Can I count on you?"

Darius's response was immediate.

"Of course, Jason. Whatever you need, I'm in."

I estimated the time to be around 10:30pm by the moon's position and Darius agreed that the likelihood of any night-time visitors was slim, especially with the guard, Faizal already posted.

"We'll wait until 1:30pm," I whispered. "By then, the guard will likely be asleep. The noise from tampering with the hinges should be enough to rouse and draw him in. You position yourself by Trevor and pretend to tend to him. I'll be to the left of the door. Once he opens the door, scream blue murder to divert his attention. Are we clear?"

His affirmative response solidified our plan. Now, all that remained was to wait for the opportune moment to act.

The next two and a half hours stretched into what felt like an eternity. With nothing but my thoughts for company, I found myself absentmindedly twirling the small, razor-sharp blade, watching its steel catch the moonlight. Every so often, I would close my eyes, visualizing the guard's entrance just as I had planned it. Confidence in Darius's ability to follow through buoyed my hopes for the plan's success. This guard, Faizal, was the one responsible for the rocket that had killed Alex. He would find no mercy at my hands. *No, there would be no mercy at all.*

My body ached, prompting me to massage my limbs in anticipation of the imminent action. The swelling around my left eye had started to subside, though I knew I bore the marks of a rough ordeal. Meanwhile, Darius sat with an expression mingled with hope and fear, and his resolve was both heartening and burdensome. The weight of his expectations was a heavy load, especially with the escape's success far from guaranteed. The odds were decidedly against us, and the image of being shot out of the water by a trigger-happy crew member of the Kaminski vessel haunted me.

But the alternative, remaining captive to these madmen was unthinkable. The thought of retribution for Alex's death overshadowed any concern for the ransom money. My primary objective was the safety of the hostages, and it was that which guided my every decision. As the moment to act drew near, the building adrenalin lent some clarity and focus, a familiar sensation to those trained for combat. Watching my fellow captives, I knew their commitment was total and they understood staying meant certain death for them. The specifics of the takedown were mine alone to know. There was no need to alarm Darius further; he just needed to execute his role. After mentally rehearsing one last time, I approached him, whispering,

"Get ready and get into position by Trevor now."

He moved without hesitation, taking his place as I positioned myself by the heavy steel door. In the oppressive humidity, I gave a final thumbs up before setting to work. Crouched down, and with the tip of my buckle knife, I began to tamper with the door's giant lower hinge, producing a soft but distinct sound of metal scraping against metal. I continued this for a few minutes until I heard a sleepy grunt from beyond the door. *He's heard you now, Green.* Shortly after, the sound of scuffling sand and the guard's sleepy mutterings in Somali reached my ears. Faizal had heard the scraping noise and was about to respond. My plan was unfolding just as intended.

Faizal barked an angry question in Somali, and I saw Darius turn to face him from his crouched position near Trevor. As instructed, he let out a panicked cry for help, suggesting Trevor was dead or near death. The first thing to appear, as expected, was the AK-47.

Poised like a coiled spring, I waited until the guard fully exposed himself in the doorway before striking. My kick, swift as a piston, connected with the side of the raised weapon, sending it flying across the cell toward the far wall, spinning as it went. The blow broke the man's forefinger caught in the trigger guard, and his yell of pain was quickly muffled by the palm of my left hand as I gripped him and pulled him towards me from behind. Without hesitation, I plunged the blade of the buckle knife into the side of his neck, feeling the shock and pain ripple through his body.

Faizal began to buck and kick with surprising strength, but I continued the rapid stabbing motion, each time the blade sank to my knuckles I twisted it before pulling it free once more. A loud, squelching sound accompanied each withdrawal, and I felt torrents of hot blood wash over my hand and forearm. Within fifteen seconds of frenzied stabbing, Faizal's body went limp, his struggles ceased, and his life ebbed away.

52

Chapter Fifty-Two.

Sleep eluded Omar that night. Restlessly, he tossed on his filthy mattress, the oppressive heat and humidity amplifying his discomfort. His mind was a whirlwind of scenarios, still reeling from the afternoon's brutal violence. He questioned why fate had paired him with the paranoid and violent Suleiman Abdi. So far, it had been nothing but torment and the promised payday had yet to materialize. Yes, three million dollars was at stake, but everything had spiralled out of control. Now, they were burdened with three hostages instead of two and one medic was dead. Omar couldn't fathom how things had deteriorated so rapidly.

By 8:00pm in the evening, Omar had started to drown his sorrows in cheap gin, his favoured escape. The alcohol slid down easily, offering a temporary respite amid the chaos and the nearby sounds of celebration. But Omar found no reason to rejoice. He longed only to collect his pay and escape the Somali coast for his beloved Mogadishu. The hostages' lives meant nothing to him, and his sole focus was the money. However, Suleiman Abdi's erratic and paranoid behaviour was a constant worry. Omar wondered how long it would be before he received his payment and permission to leave.

The ordeal seemed endless, as if he had been stranded on the Puntland coast for years. Drink after drink, Omar numbed himself until he realized the need for clarity in the morning. Staggering from his hut, he ambled toward the waterline, welcoming the cool ocean breeze. Lifting his robe and unzipping his trousers, Omar relieved himself, swaying slightly. Once finished, he took a moment to appreciate the moon's reflection on the ocean—a rare instance of tranquility amid the tumult.

The party's music persisted, but Omar found solitude by the beach. Venturing closer to the water, he crossed a low wall near the old factory area and sat, gazing at the dull grey water bathed in moonlight. Breathing in the salty air, he experienced a fleeting sense of peace in an otherwise chaotic existence.

After about ten minutes, Omar stood, stretched and returned to the tin shack he'd called home for far too long.

"Sleep," he muttered as he entered, "I must sleep. There's much to do tomorrow. Sleep, I must sleep."

53

Chapter Fifty-Three.

Eventually, I dropped the man's dying body onto the concrete floor of the cell. Apart from a few weak twitches, he lay still, a pool of blood expanding around his head and upper torso. As he died, it came as no surprise to hear Darius retching and vomiting, unaccustomed as he was to such extreme violence. His body had an instant and uncontrollable reaction to the sight. Once he had emptied his stomach, he wiped his mouth, stood up straight and looked at me with wide eyes.

"What now?" he said quietly.

"Now, we get the fuck out of here," I replied.

Wasting no time, I walked to the far end of the cell and picked up the man's battered AK47. I checked it over once to ensure it was serviceable and found it to be in working condition. This was common among these tough, Soviet-made weapons. Their durability made them very attractive to African armies, bandits, and the like. Finally, I stepped up to the cell door, carrying the gun and looked around. The moon was higher in the sky and would provide us with much-needed visibility as we made our way down to the harbour. Our biggest encumbrance was, of course, Trevor, who would need help, if not carrying, down to the harbour. But there was nothing else we could do about that, we had to get him out. Seeing the coast was clear and that there was no one else around, I rushed back into the cell and rummaged through the pockets of the man I had just killed. The first thing I retrieved was his cell phone. I pushed the on button, searched for a signal, and found one. A Somali sole provider showed on the screen. Sadly, I had not memorized any of the crucial numbers I had before my equipment and phone were stolen by the men at the failed hostage rescue attempt. But this was something that might come in handy for me, so I pocketed it immediately after muting the sound. Next, I found the keys to the padlocks, which I grabbed. Finally, I stood up, looked over at Darius and down at Trevor who had brought himself into a sitting position. His eyes alternated between looking up at me and down at the dead man lying in an ever-increasing pool of blood. The blood appeared black in the shafts of moonlight that filtered through the bars on the small window.

"Right," I said decisively, "It's time to go. Let's do this. We're going to have to help him walk, one arm over each of our shoulders. If that fails, we're going to have to carry him. The distance down to the water isn't that far, maybe a kilometre. When we reach the harbour, we may need to hide out for a bit while I find some fuel and perhaps some other resources. Then, my plan is to steal a boat and head out to the Kaminski vessel. As you can hear, the men down there are celebrating. Hopefully, that will keep them occupied while we make our escape. In the meantime, I'm going to lock our friend Faizal here inside and hopefully, we can escape unnoticed. With any luck, it'll be late morning before anyone realizes we're gone. And when they find their dead comrade in here, hopefully, we'll be aboard the Kaminski ship."

Seemingly approving of my plan, I saw both Darius and Trevor nod their heads in agreement. It was good to have the support of the men I was trying to help.

"Trevor, can you stand up?" I asked.

"I can try," he whispered.

But then I saw Darius go over and help him stand. The man was clearly very weak, but his spirit was still alive and his desire to escape was clear. As Darius escorted Trevor out of the cell door, I shifted the dead man's legs briefly to get him out of the line of sight of the window before following both men out. Once there, I turned around and re-locked the padlocks, keeping the keys in my pocket. To anyone approaching, it would appear that the cell was locked as usual, and the prisoners inside. There was nothing out of the ordinary.

Next, I turned around and faced the coast, took a deep breath, and spoke.

"Right," I said, "Let's do this. We must move quietly."

"Yeah, we're ready," whispered Darius and there was a nod from Trevor.

I grabbed Trevor's left arm and pulled it around my neck, while Darius did the same on the other side. At first, our progress was a bit clumsy, but soon enough we fell into an easy pacing pattern. We covered a good amount of ground quietly at an acceptable speed.

It was after about 100 metres or so that I whispered to Darius that it might be safer for us to move off the hard-packed road and into the dunes on the right. This would offer us some form of cover should anyone be walking up the road from the settlement.

The sound of wild celebrations grew louder and louder as we slowly made our way down towards the settlement in the moonlight. Everything I had memorized from the satellite photographs became clear to me and although my body ached from the beating I had received, I felt the familiar tingle of adrenalin in my arms and legs as I realized we were getting closer and closer to danger. My initial plan of skirting around the settlement and avoiding going anywhere near it seemed to be working. Darius was moving well with no complaints, as was Trevor, in between us, although by then he was mostly being carried by us by his shoulders. Still, it was admirable that he kept quiet through the whole ordeal and simply allowed things to go on as they did. It was as we became parallel with the settlement and the music was at its loudest that I heard a metal door slam, a gunshot going off and two men shouting. Instantly, I whispered to Darius to get down, which we did immediately and lay face down in the sand. Looking back towards the settlement we saw two men had emerged from one of the metal shacks, both armed and both clearly drunk. They were having some kind of disagreement and one had fired his weapon into the air. The shouting continued as their argument progressed, but eventually, both men stumbled off in their separate directions, clearly drunk and heading home for the night.

I watched them as they walked in their flowing robes in the moonlight, carrying the dreaded AK47s like the one I too was carrying. I knew these men were responsible for the death of Alex and I gritted my teeth as I watched them disappear into their respective accommodations. I waited a few more minutes before giving the all-clear and telling Darius to stand up.

Once again, we had made good progress towards the harbour and skirting around on the right had been successful. We had run into no guards on the way. It was when we were a good 100 metres past the settlement that the breeze from the ocean became stronger, and I could smell the salt in the air much more clearly than before. I could also hear the soft sounds of the waves crashing into the sand.

"Right," I said, "I'm going to leave you here and skirt around down towards the harbour past where I was supposed to pick you up today. Once I get there, I'm going to identify a boat on which we can escape and I'm going to scout out some fuel and make sure that we have enough to get to the Kaminski ship. I want you to stay here, remain quiet and lie flat. This is very important."

"Yes, of course," said Darius and I watched as Trevor Nichol nodded weakly.

"Good," I said. "I'm going to go now. By my reckoning, we've got about four hours before sunrise. There's plenty of time for me to do what I need to do. I'll be back shortly, hopefully with good news and we can get the fuck out of here."

"OK," said Darius, nodding keenly.

I stood up quietly and made my way further down towards the sound of the waves. The breeze coming in off the ocean was pleasant on my skin, and had it not been for the appalling situation I found myself in, the walk may well have been enjoyable. But the burden of responsibility on my shoulders was too great, and my body ached from the beating.

It was about five minutes later when I saw the gunmetal grey of the ocean in front of me and heard the repetitive whooshing of the waves. Knowing I was close enough to the waterline, I turned left and made my way, crouched over in the moonlight towards where I knew the boats were moored. I moved slowly, always aware of what was around me and doing my best to stay covered by dunes and shadows.

Up ahead, I saw the derelict factory in front of which the terrible events of the afternoon had taken place. I knew that the structure would give me cover on the way to the harbour, so I moved diagonally inland towards it, quietly padding my way up the soft sand in the moonlight. Once I was within a few metres of the derelict building, I stopped, turned around and looked at my surroundings. There was no one there and the only sound was that of the pounding music from the settlement further inland and the crashing of the small waves behind me. *Good, this is going well, Green.* Slowly, I made my way across the front of the derelict factory. But it was as I came to the front left corner that I heard it: a human being humming a tune. I froze in my tracks, the adrenalin coursing through my veins. The sound of the man was close, and I could not for the life of me think how I had missed him, how I had not seen him. Perhaps he had been there all along. If I had not heard the humming, I would have walked out straight into his vision and God only knows what would have happened then.

With my back to the derelict building, I inched towards the corner and then poked my head around briefly to see who was there. It was a face I recognized immediately, different from the normal thin Somali face structure. The man's face was oval and his black, curly hair was in an Afro style. His robe was blue and flowing and he sat on a low sea wall, staring listlessly at the ocean. His body appeared to sway back and forth as he sat as if the breeze was blowing him. But it was then that I realized he was drunk. It was a face I had drummed into my consciousness over the past days: the face of the man who was the interpreter for Suleiman Abdi, the link between Kaminski and the kidnappers. It was the face of Omar.

Filthy fucker, I thought to myself. Here was the man whom many people had trusted to resolve the situation. Here was the man who had turned his back on a deal, allowing everything to descend into appalling violence and cold-blooded murder.

And there he was, completely unaware of my presence, not ten metres from where I stood, swaying in the breeze, humming a tune to himself while in the distance the wild celebration and the pounding music of the other men continued unabated into the night.

What had brought Omar here alone? What made him decide not to join the other men in their celebrations and instead apparently drink alone and sit here, staring out at the ocean in the moonlight? My mind turned over these thoughts and questions as I stared at him, and a burning hatred rose in my stomach. But it was then that I saw him stand up and as he did so, he swayed yet again, the alcohol coursing through his veins. He was on the move, and I quickly ducked behind the building once again. The next time I looked, Omar had stepped over the low sea wall and was headed towards a solitary metal shack that was positioned not far from the derelict factory. I remembered seeing this building from satellite pictures, and now it appeared that this was Omar's dwelling. Bolstered by the fact that the man was extremely drunk and unlikely to be aware of my presence, I moved down the side of the building to watch his progress as he moved in the moonlight. Eventually, he reached the door, pulled it open and stumbled into his dwelling leaving the door ajar.

I watched as he fell sideways onto a bed and lay there motionless, with the door still partially open. The dull yellow light of a paraffin lamp glowed on the inside. Crouching down in the shadows, with my gun at the ready, I watched him as he drifted off to sleep.

You need this man, Green. You need his knowledge. He can help you. He will help you find the best vessel to carry the hostages out to the Kaminski ship. He is well-versed with the area and the running of this encampment, and he can advise you. He could be of great help. Instead of you just making your way to the harbour and randomly picking out some derelict, he may well be able to help you, Green. You need to think about this. And what's more, if you were to take him prisoner, it would be some kind of justice for young Alex if this man, Omar, is tried in a Kenyan court for piracy. The man's drunk clearly and he doesn't seem to be in any physical state to resist me taking him prisoner.

By then, I knew what I needed to do, and I had already decided that I would take him prisoner. His solitary shack was far enough from the main settlement for me to do it without anyone knowing. My plan would be to apprehend him, silence him and take him down to the harbour. From there, I would choose the vessel I needed, fuel it up, tie and gag Omar, leave him in the vessel, and return to collect Trevor and Darius. From there, we would make our way back to the boat and quietly slip out of the harbour without anyone being any the wiser. With any luck, we would be at the Kaminski vessel by 8:00 or 9:00 in the morning, and I would have completed my mission, sadly, with only the loss of young Alex. *Yes, Green, this is a good plan. This man can help you. Go get him!* It was some 10 minutes later when I realized that the drunk Omar was completely comatose from alcohol. He had not shifted once and the door of his shack, still slightly ajar, showed him still lying on the filthy mattress where he had collapsed. I knew it was time to move. *Let's do it, Green.* I removed the buckle knife from my belt, slung the AK47 over my right shoulder and with the bloodied blade sticking through my fingers, I crouched down and crossed the littered sand in the moonlight towards the door of the metal shack. The bulk of the building of the derelict factory had prevented any of the sea breeze and once again, it was humid. The sound of the pounding music from the nearby celebration was repetitive and maddening at the same time.

Every now and then, there was cheering, hooting and the occasional, random gunshot. It appeared like the men were fully occupied and the party would continue well into the night.

Soon enough, I arrived at the door of Omar's shack. I turned with my back to the front left wall and stood there to wait and listen for any movement, but there was none. All that I could hear was a steady grumbling sound that was Omar snoring loudly in his alcoholic stupor. It was some minutes later and there had been no movement at all, that I decided to make my move. Turning around, I walked silently on the sand and entered through the door, pulling it slowly and quietly behind me until it was closed. The interior of the metal shack was like a sauna and the stench of body odour was overwhelming. It came as a physical shock to me as I stood there and for a moment, I wished I had left the door open. Omar lay as he had done since he had returned from the sea wall, on his side and snoring loudly and repetitively. On a makeshift table next to his filthy mattress was a bottle of what appeared to be clear spirit, perhaps gin. The man had drunk the entire bottle. I knew that when I did wake him, it would come as one hell of a surprise.

With the sound of the nearby celebration muffled by the metal walls of the shack, I crossed the floor towards the bed until I stood over the figure of the sleeping man. Once again, I was reminded of the terrible body odour emanating from him; it was as if he had not bathed in months. Slowly, I crouched down until my face was only two feet from his. The repetitive snoring sounded like a burst tyre. With the blade of the buckle knife protruding from my knuckles, I reached forward and held the razor-sharp steel against the side of his neck. At first, there was no response, but after adding a bit of pressure, Omar's eyes opened suddenly, and he stared at me face-to-face in the yellow light of the paraffin lamp. His bloodshot eyes were wide as saucers and filled with horror as he stared at me in total disbelief.

"Good evening," I said quietly.

54

CHAPTER FIFTY-FOUR.

Sleep did not come easy for Suleiman Abdi that evening. Instead, he found himself constantly pacing the front room of his mud-brick dwelling, his mind buzzing with possibilities, problems and potential solutions—but even more, potential problems. Yes, there had been the success of acquiring the three million U.S. dollars. There was no doubting that fact. The box containing the cash was locked in a strong room adjacent to the front room he was now sitting in. On more than five occasions, he had unlocked the heavy steel door, entered the room, opened the crate and fondled the giant pile of money, his fingers flicking through the bundled banknotes—crisp $100 notes from the United States of America. A fortune by any man's book.

After reassuring himself at least three or four times, he told himself he must go and rest. But rest was something that did not come that night. Instead, he rose and brewed himself more green tea, listening to the sound of the men celebrating in the distance. This was something he would not begrudge the men. They had worked faithfully for him for the past three or four months, had carried out his every instruction and had done so very well. No, he thought, they must have a celebration. Of course, they should. They have worked hard.

But paramount in Suleiman Abdi's mind was the fact that the hostage exchange had gone terribly wrong. It had been the plane in the sky, which he had thought was a drone, that had got his paranoia raging. Once again, alas, it had not gone as planned and the hostage rescue boat had been blown up, along with one of their men in the process. Still, this was not a concern for Suleiman Abdi. The concern was that there were now three prisoners in his charge—three prisoners which he needed to get rid of.

Now, in his mind, there were only two ways of doing that. The first would be to release them. This could possibly be done by placing them somewhere on the Somali coast, contacting their people from Kaminski and informing them that they had been dropped somewhere. This was a possibility that Suleiman Abdi had gone through in his mind several times. But deep down inside, he knew that this option was fraught with possible danger. By then, the man who had come to collect the hostages had seen too much. He had seen the encampment; he had seen the layout, and he was aware of many of the functions of the group of bandits. In Suleiman Abdi's mind, leaving the hostages alive and on the beach somewhere to the south or the north posed not only a danger to his operation but a direct threat to his own life.

Option No. 2, which was becoming more and more attractive in his mind, was to simply eliminate the three hostages and dump their bodies in the ocean. A clean and swift cull carried out the next morning and the hassle of keeping the three men prisoners and the constant back-and-forth with Kaminski would be instantly over and forgotten. All lines of communication with the people at Kaminski would be cut. The $3,000,000 would be his. He would make his payments to the men and move on to the next project in his life. Of course, he would do so with an extremely large amount of cash, and his future would be secured.

So, it was these two options and this decision that completely occupied Suleiman Abdi's mind that night and it had been preventing him from being able to rest and sleep. It was at around 2:00am in the morning when Suleiman Abdi finally cursed to himself in his native Somali dialect, but at last, he had come to a decision.

The decision was that there would be a clean break and the three prisoners would be killed first thing in the morning. Feeling the need to give this order before he retired to bed, Suleiman Abdi walked over to his desk, lifted his cell phone, scrolled through until he found the number for Omar, and rang it.

55

Chapter Fifty-Five.

"What happened to our deal, you filthy piece of shit?" I whispered into his sweating ear.

Omar, with wide, terrified eyes, gulped and said nothing. I applied further pressure with the buckle knife to his neck, and it was enough to make him change his mind.

"It was Suleiman," he pleaded. "Suleiman messed the whole thing up."

"A lot of people trusted you, Omar," I said. "Everyone at Kaminski was relying on you. We're talking about months and months of protracted negotiations which you allowed to fall to pieces in a matter of seconds. Not only that, one of my people is dead thanks to your blunder. And you still have the $3,000,000. You can imagine I'm not feeling very happy at this stage."

"I tried," pleaded Omar and I smelled the gin on his breath. "I did my best, please believe me, Mr. Green. Please. It was Suleiman, he is a madman. He is so paranoid; it is almost impossible to work with him. For months, I've been trying to get this across to the man at Kaminski. It has been a living hell for me as well. Please understand."

"I don't give a fuck what kind of hell you've been going through, Omar. It's nothing compared to what you've put your prisoners through, and that of their families. It's amazing they're still alive, given the treatment they've been given under your watch. I hold you personally responsible."

"What can I do to help you?" pleaded the terrified man.

"Well," I said, "as you can see, we are no longer in your filthy cell. We will be leaving here tonight, and you are going to help us do that. Do you understand?"

"Yes, yes, of course," said Omar, his eyes reflecting the realization that he might escape with his life. "Anything I can do to help you, of course, I shall do it."

His voice was now slightly stronger, it was clear that Omar had become sober rather quickly after realizing who it was who had visited him in the night.

"I need a boat. A good, strong, fast boat," I said. "And I need fuel. And, if possible, some medical supplies. But most importantly, I need a boat, and I need it now."

"Yes, yes, of course. There are a few boats down at the harbour. I know of one which you could use, but there is a problem."

"What fucking problem?" I growled, forcing the blade closer into his neck.

"Please, please, Mr. Green, please do not cut me!" he whimpered.

"Tell me the problem, Omar, or I will cut you."

"The fuel, sir. All the fuel stock is in the armoury. Suleiman is very careful to guard it. All fuel is kept with the guns and ammunition in the armoury."

"When you talk about the armoury, do you mean the building next to Suleiman's residence?"

"Yes, yes," said Omar. "That's it."

"And why can we not go there? Skirt around the settlement, enter the armoury, and collect the fuel now? Why can we not do that?"

"It is under lock and key, Sir," said Omar, his voice trembling. "Suleiman is the one who keeps the keys. He has the money, the $3,000,000, in his house, but the fuel and all of the guns are kept in the armoury."

"I don't give a fuck about the money. Do you understand me, Omar?" I spoke. "You can keep the money. What I want is to get my people out of here and back to safety. That is my only concern. Are we clear?"

"Yes, yes, it's clear. But we... there is no fuel kept in the boats, that is for sure. We will need to go and collect it, and to do that, we will have to go through Suleiman."

"Very well," I growled. "If that is what we must do, then we will do exactly that. But let me warn you now, Omar. Let me give you one very serious warning. If you are lying to me, if you are trying to pull the wool over my eyes, or if I even suspect that you are trying to hoodwink me, I will not think twice and I will cut your fucking throat. Understood?"

"Yes, yes, Mr. Green, of course. I understand, and I will help you.

"There's one thing you need to understand right now, Omar," I said "Your men have killed a friend of mine and your life means very little to me now. You put one foot out of step, and I will not hesitate to kill you. Make sure of that."

"Yes, yes," he whispered, his eyes shining with a sparkle of hope that he might live through the night.

But it was then that the cell phone on the makeshift table next to the filthy bed vibrated. It was a thin buzzing sound on the cheap wooden surface, covered in crumbs and spilt alcohol. My eyes darted to the right to look at the device, and the screen was illuminated—one word was clearly visible. The name of the caller was Suleiman.

I let it ring for three seconds, watching it before my eyes went back to Omar's, with the blade still pressed against the side of his neck by his jugular vein.

"Talk of the devil," I said. "Looks like Suleiman would like to talk to you right away. Now, Omar, I'm going to allow you to sit up. I want you to answer this phone. I want you to talk to Suleiman as you normally would. I want you to talk in your native Somali dialect, calmly and normally. Remember, you step out of line, I kill you. I want you to find out what he wants. Are we clear?"

"Yes, yes," said Omar.

"Right," I said, as I removed the blade from his neck.

There was a drop of blood on his skin. I stood up, took the AK47 from around my shoulder, pointed it at Omar's head and spoke.

"Sit up now," I said.

As the now sober Omar sat up on the filthy mattress, I reached behind me and pulled over a crude wooden stool. I sat down, with the muzzle of the barrel inches from Omar's face. His eyes, bloodshot and wide as saucers, he lifted the receiver and stared at the screen.

"Answer it, you cunt. Answer it now, and remember, one wrong move and you're dead."

Omar's trembling hand moved towards the phone and with a hesitant touch, he swiped to answer the call. His voice, barely above a whisper, began speaking in Somali, the words flowing in a steady stream. My finger rested on the trigger, ready to act at the slightest hint of betrayal. This conversation could determine the fate of our escape plan and every syllable uttered by Omar was critical. As he spoke, I watched closely for any sign of deception or panic that might indicate a deviation from our agreed-upon plan. The stakes were high, and the tension in the room was palpable. Omar's fate, as well as our own, hinged on the outcome of this conversation. The mumbled conversation lasted no more than ten seconds before Omar hung up, placed the phone on the bedside table and turned to look at me with great fear in his eyes.

"What did he say?" I asked. "What does he want?"

"He wants to see me," Omar replied. "I have no idea why."

"Is it normal for him to ask to see you in the middle of the night like this?" I asked.

"No, Sir. No, Mr. Green, it is not normal at all. Normally, I have a meeting every morning with Suleiman and that is it. Please believe me when I tell you I have no idea why he wants to see me."

I paused as I thought about this new and unexpected development. Given that the keys for the armoury and the fuel storage lay with Suleiman himself, this surprise phone call presented an opportunity for me. Turning this over in my mind time and again, I finally spoke.

"What about the armoury?" I asked. "And the fuel, how secure is it? Can I break in there?"

"There are two heavy padlocks," Omar said. "They are very strong and will be difficult to break without making a lot of noise. The only way to enter is with the keys."

Having seen the padlocks on the cell that the hostages and I had been kept in, I knew that it would indeed be almost impossible to enter the armoury without the keys Omar mentioned. The fact that Suleiman wanted to see Omar remained an opportunity, number one to get the keys and number two to silence Suleiman.

With my thought process complete and my decision made, I spoke again.

"And how will we go to his residence, Omar?" I asked. "If we are to go together, is there a way to get there in the darkness without being seen?"

Omar cleared his throat, his face now showing that he had sobered up entirely. With wide eyes, he answered,

"I'm sure you know, Mr. Green, Suleiman's residence is some distance from where the men are celebrating tonight. The armoury is next door. If we skirt around the left of the camp, avoiding the thoroughfare where the men are celebrating, we can reach Suleiman's house in relative darkness."

"Are you telling me the truth, Omar?" I asked with narrowed eyes.

"As God is my witness, Mr. Green, I tell you no lie," said Omar, his voice panicking. "I can lead you there now. We will be walking in darkness almost all the way. The only time you'll be exposed to any light will be when we approach the front door of Suleiman's house."

"Very well," I said, glancing around the room. "Do you have some spare robes for me to wear?"

"Yes," he said. "In the corner, on the clothes hanger, is a spare robe."

I had no wish to make my way through an enemy encampment wearing what I was wearing. The more I could do to fit into the environment and appear like one of the other men, the better and the less chance there would be of me being discovered. I stood up, keeping the gun aimed at Omar and walked over to the corner of the metal shack where he had indicated. Sure enough, on a wire coat hanger pegged into the wall was a cream-coloured robe, full-length. With the gun still aimed, I pulled it over my head until my head showed through the neck hole, then fed my left arm through, passing the weapon to my left hand and still aiming at Omar's head. I fed my right arm through the top of the robe, then pulled it down until the hem of it was around my ankles.

"Right," I hissed. "Now, Omar, you and I are going to take a little walk in the moonlight. As you said, we are going to skirt around the left of the encampment and we're going to visit Mr. Suleiman Abdi. You make one wrong move, and I will kill you. Do you understand?"

"Yes, yes, Mr. Green, I understand," he replied.

"When we get there, I want you to enter as you normally do and do not be tempted to try and raise the alarm in any way. You know what will happen if you do."

"Yes, I understand, Mr. Green. Everything should appear as normal."

"Right," I said. "Let's go."

The sight of two robed figures, one with an AK-47 slung over his shoulder, was not unusual or unexpected in the camp. Sticking to our original plan, I followed a few feet behind the terrified figure of Omar as we left the hut and headed left, skirting around the central area of the bandit camp. Up ahead, not a hundred metres away, stood the squat, low, mud-brick residence of Suleiman Abdi, a yellow glow coming from the windows on the side and the front of the building.

"Keep moving as you normally would," I grated at him.

Omar said nothing but obeyed my every command as we padded along. Thankfully, there were no interruptions and the sound of the celebrations continued in the distance with shouting and cheering. *So far, so good*, I thought. *So far, so good*. It was some minutes later when we came up alongside the building that was Suleiman Abdi's house. Omar stopped as we reached the corner of the building, turned back and stared at me with a terrified look on his face.

"Carry on," I growled. "Carry on as usual and remember, I'm right behind you. Any tricks and you're done for."

Omar nodded jerkily and turned back, proceeding towards the front door. Once he got there, he turned, looked at me briefly and then knocked three times in quick succession on the heavy wood of the door. There was a brief pause, and we heard a tired-sounding, guttural grunt from the interior. With another quick look at me, Omar reached forward, turned the handle and pushed the door inwards. He paused briefly and just to give him a bit of a nudge, I jammed the muzzle of the AK-47 into his lower back. This was enough to prompt him to walk in, which he did quietly and solemnly.

Suleiman Abdi was sitting on the far-left side of the room on a large cushion. In front of him was an elaborate tea set that looked Arabic in origin and he was busy stirring a clear glass of steaming green tea. I closed the door behind me quietly, noticing with surprise that the elderly man still had not looked up or acknowledged my presence. Once again, I jammed the barrel of the gun into Omar's back, and he stumbled forward. The sudden movement caused Suleiman Abdi to look up, his stern, mask-like face suddenly contorted in anger and fear. Almost immediately, a strange, guttural wail emanated from his lips, and he dived to the left in an attempt to reach the AK-47 that was propped up against the wall. Wasting no time, I slammed the butt of my own rifle into the side of Omar's head, knocking him to the right, then launched myself forward over the cushions and kicked the silver tray and its contents at the seated old man. The boiling tea flew in all directions, soaking his midriff and stopping him in his tracks.

Again, there was another guttural wail and a sudden flailing of his thin arms, but I had reached him in time and there was no way he was going to reach the weapon in time to pose any danger to me. Grabbing him by the front of his tunic with my left hand, I forced him back against the wall and held the gun to his face. Now that I had cornered him, my eyes darted to the right to see the sprawled-out figure of Omar moaning on the polished floor of the front room.

"Get up," I hissed at him. "Get up now."

Omar slowly lifted himself onto his hands and then his knees and staggered over towards where I was seated.

"Sit down," I said.

Omar did exactly as I said and sat in front of the clearly enraged Suleiman Abdi. A look of defeat covered both men's faces.

"Keys," I said to Omar. "Ask him where the keys are, now."

Omar, with an apologetic and terrified look on his face, burst out into some babbled conversation in guttural Somali.

"Keep it short," I growled. "I want the keys, nothing else. We're not here to talk bullshit. Are you clear? Keys only. That's what I want."

Omar nodded furiously and then realized that he had better adhere to my instructions. There was another quick utterance and then silence. I turned to see how Suleiman would respond, but there was only silence. Suleiman Abdi's hawklike face was a mask of defiance and fury.

"He is refusing to hand over the keys," said Omar, his voice trembling.

"Very well," I replied. "Tell him that if he doesn't give me the keys now, I will cut off one of his fingers."

As I said these words, Omar's eyes widened. It was clear that this sort of communication was unheard of between him and Suleiman Abdi, but I had no qualms about carrying out my threat.

"Tell him now," I muttered, my jaw set

Omar babbled something out in Somali, and I turned once again to look at Suleiman, but his face remained unchanged and defiant. Wasting no time, I transferred the AK-47 to my left hand, keeping the muzzle close to Suleiman's head. Next, I pulled the belt buckle knife from its sheath. Turning to Omar, I ordered,

"Take his hand, Omar. Take his hand and put it down here on the floor in front of me. Hold it down. One wrong move, and I'll kill you. Do you understand?"

"Yes, yes," he said, his voice trembling with fear.

It was then that I noticed the pool of liquid that had formed around Omar; the man was so terrified he had lost control of his bladder. The smell permeated the humid interior of the mud-brick building.

"Do it now," I said.

Omar reached forward and grabbed the skinny arm of his master, placing the hand in front of me on the ceramic tile.

"Spread his fingers," I ordered him. "Do it now."

Omar did so and as he did, I looked at Suleiman's face, which remained strangely defiant. Wasting no time, I brought the razor-sharp blade of the buckle knife down in front of the first knuckle of Suleiman Abdi's forefinger. The bone and skin broke, and the sound was like a twig snapping. Suleiman's hand jerked backwards, leaving the severed finger exactly where it had been. Suddenly, there was an unholy howling sound emanating from Suleiman's mouth, which had become a perfect circle in the thin mass of his jet-black face.

"Keys now, Omar," I commanded, my voice cutting through the racket.

Omar, sitting in the puddle of his own urine, was a pitiful sight. He launched into a pleading monologue, babbling in Somali. Suleiman Abdi, however, sat with a stony expression, a scarlet stain growing on his midriff where he clutched the hand with the severed finger. Finally, overcome, he blurted out a series of instructions in his guttural voice.

"Over there," Omar managed to say, turning to his right to eye a small chest of drawers that looked like an antique. "The keys are in the top drawer."

"Go and get them. And no funny moves," I warned him sternly.

Omar stood up, the lower half of his tunic soaking wet where he had pissed himself in fear. As he moved, his clothes made a wet, rustling sound. While I kept my eyes on his progress, I missed Suleiman Abdi's deception. Although it appeared he was clutching his right hand within his tunic, he had lifted a fold of fabric to retrieve a curved Arabian dagger hidden in a sheath on his belt. With only three functioning fingers and his thumb, he gripped the ornate handle of the dagger. With unexpected speed for a man of his age, he swung it towards my face. The first thing I noticed was the flash of the razor-sharp steel, but my reflexes were quick. I instantly raised my left hand, blocking his lunge with the butt of the AK-47. His thin, bony wrist hit the Russian weapon, and I heard a cracking sound as his bones split. The dagger rattled to the floor. Had I not been quick enough to notice his trick, there's no doubt he would have planted the blade deep into my face. Infuriated by this insult and acting completely on impulse, I reached forward with the open palm of my right hand and gripped the man by his thin face.

Without a second thought, I slammed his head as hard as I could back into the hard mud brick wall. What followed was the sound of an unripe watermelon being crushed as his skull hit the wall. Unfortunately for Suleiman Abdi, that was all it took. His limp body slumped forward, the bones in his hips making a popping sound as he fell. I stared down, hardly able to believe the sight before me. The blow had completely smashed the back of Suleiman Abdi's head, leaving nothing but a flaccid bag of shattered bone. There was a soft spluttering sound as his bowels voided, and a few minor twitches before life finally left him, and Suleiman Abdi was well and truly dead.

Omar, having witnessed this flash of violence, started trembling, a heavy metal ring of keys in his hand. Tears began to flow down his face and his body shook uncontrollably. With Suleiman dead, I leapt to my feet and strode over to where Omar stood, trembling and crying.

"There's no time for that, you fool. Let's go, now. We're heading to the armoury. Do you understand me?" I demanded.

"Yes, yes," he whimpered.

I grabbed him by the back of his collar and forced him towards the front door of the residence. Once there, I whispered in his ear once again,

"Remember, Omar, one wrong move, and you'll end up like your friend Suleiman. Are we clear?"

"Yes, yes, we are clear," he replied.

I placed the rifle over my right shoulder and jabbed the blade of the buckle knife into Omar's lower back to remind him that this was no time for fun and games. Quickly and quietly, we moved out of the light in front of the building and into the shadows, heading towards the armoury building some 20 metres to the right. Thankfully, it was hidden from much of the light of the nearby celebrations and the other shacks where the men were partying. Upon arrival, it was clear that Omar had not been lying when he had spoken of the two extremely heavy padlocks that bolted the windowless building shut. I handed him the heavy metal ring and spoke,

"Open them now."

Omar wasted no time. His shaking hands fumbled slightly as the keys jangled quietly while he opened the first padlock. Once done, he leaned over and continued with the second. Finally, with both padlocks opened, he pushed the door inward, and we were greeted by darkness. Seeing this as a problem, I pulled his cell phone from my pocket, handed it to him and whispered,

"Turn the torch on. I need to see what I'm doing here."

Omar quickly flicked the screen and within a few seconds, the interior of the armoury was illuminated by the torch of the cell phone. Without wasting time, I snatched the device from him and looked around. Indeed, Omar had not misled us; this was where much of the fuel, weapons, and ammunition were stored. To the left stood a giant raised bowser, which I estimated held 5000 litres of petrol. Next to it was another identical bowser, seemingly filled with diesel. Below these were about 40 old yellow 20-litre containers, stained and battered. They might have seen better days, but I knew they would serve their purpose just as well as new ones.

"I'm going to need at least 150 litres of petrol," I stated firmly. "Do you hear me, Omar? I don't want any diesel. We need a fast boat."

"Yes, yes, Mr. Green. There is a fast boat that runs on petrol only. I can show it to you," Omar replied, his voice still shaky.

"We have another problem," I said, contemplating our next steps. "These containers are 20 litres each. There's no way we're going to move ten of them down to the harbour, just the two of us. We need a vehicle. Where is the pickup that was used earlier?"

"All of the vehicles are behind Suleiman's house," Omar said, his voice still trembling.

"Do you know how to drive, Omar?"

"Yes, yes, I do drive."

"Right," I said decisively. "Let's go and get a vehicle."

Closing the door quietly behind me, I nudged Omar to the left, around the building and into the darkness beyond. Up ahead, I could see the moonlight glinting off what was left of the chrome on the bumper of the old pickup.

"Quickly," I muttered forcefully as we crossed the litter-strewn sand towards it.

As we arrived, I wasted no time in instructing Omar to jump in the front seat of the vehicle while I skirted around the front and opened the passenger door to climb in. Once settled, I found the truck key on the heavy metal ring that held the armoury keys, removed it from the latch, and handed it to Omar.

"Keep the revs low and the lights off. I don't want to attract any attention." I said.

"Yes, yes," he replied, his hands trembling as he fitted the key into the ignition.

The sound of the diesel engine lurching to life made me cringe; it was so loud it could attract unwanted attention. Thankfully, there was none, and it turned out that Omar was indeed a smooth driver. He reversed the vehicle and started heading back towards the armoury in the darkness.

"Park behind the armoury where no one can see us," I instructed.

"Yes, yes, okay, I'll do that," he replied.

The short distance was covered quickly, and I told him to turn the motor off immediately. Next, we circled the building and entered the armoury once again. Thankfully, the yellow containers beneath the petrol bowser were all full, saving us a lot of time as it would have taken precious time to decant from the bowser into the containers. Noting this with satisfaction, I spoke,

"Right, I want you to carry them two at a time out of the door and put them in the back of the pickup. Are we clear?"

"Yes, we're clear," he said.

"I'll be waiting in the darkness outside. My gun will be right on you. You make a move, and I think you know what I'm going to do to you."

"Yes," he said. "I'll do it. I'll do it very quickly, Mr. Green."

"Good. Get to it," I said.

I moved into the darkness on the left-hand side of the armoury and watched as Omar began shuttling back and forth from the darkened door, each time he moved carrying 40 litres of fuel. It took no more than eight minutes for him to finish the job. Finally, he stood there, panting and sweating in the moonlight.

"There's one more thing I want to do in here," I said. "Go back into the armoury."

We walked into the dark space again and I flicked on the torch on Omar's phone. There, in the corner on the right, was an array of five RPG rocket launchers leaning on the wall, the rockets placed neatly in boxes near them, the top of one box having been jimmied open to reveal the deadly contents packed in sawdust.

"Get one of the launchers and three of those rockets and take them out," I said.

As Omar busied himself collecting the rockets and the rocket launcher, I grabbed a couple of belts of ammunition for the AK-47 I was carrying. Finally, when everything was loaded, we left the armoury. I turned to lock the door once again; there was no point in allowing the bandits access to the weapons and ammo should we be discovered during our escape. *No, that's not going to happen*, I thought as I secured the locks. Finally, we made it round to the back of the armoury to the pickup now loaded with 200 litres of fuel. Carefully, I instructed Omar to place the rocket launcher and the rockets into the back and quickly told him to jump in the front of the pickup truck once again. Once inside, I held the blade to the side of his neck and spoke,

"Now, Omar, we're going to take a very slow drive. We're going to circle around the camp, no lights, no revving, no hooting. Then we're going to go all the way around down to the harbour. Along the way, we're going to pick up the two hostages. When we get there, I will instruct you on what to do next. Okay?"

"Yes, yes," he replied clearly.

"Right," I said. "Start the vehicle."

Omar turned the key, and the sound of the old diesel engine turning over felt like it was amplified a thousand times in my ears. Surely someone would hear it in the night and our escape would be revealed to all. However, the old diesel engine did not start; instead, there was an awful lurching sound.

"Try it again," I hissed through gritted teeth.

Once again, Omar turned the key, and there was the terrible lurching sound of the engine turning over, but weaker this time. In my mind, I realized that all this effort of loading the fuel and the rocket launcher into the back of the old pickup may have been a futile waste of time. The old pickup was battered and had seen a life of abuse, so it should have been no surprise that it would fail to start. But it was at that moment that I felt Omar's phone vibrate in my left pocket.

"Wait," I whispered as I reached into the pocket and brought the device out.

I held the screen in front of my face, curious as to who would be phoning him at this late hour. But what I saw next, I could hardly believe: the name on the screen was one I recognized very well. For a moment, my world was full of doubt. *Was this really happening?* And I doubted my own sanity. Here we were, at 2:00am in the morning on the coast of Somalia and Omar was receiving a personal phone call from none other than Younis Bader in Poland. *What the fuck?* I blinked and looked at the screen again, wondering if I was seeing things. But it was real; there was no doubt the person who was phoning was Younis Bader. *What the actual fuck?* I held the phone up to the trembling figure of Omar and the glow from the screen lit up his terrified face. His eyes only widened as he saw the name of the caller.

"What the fuck is going on here, Omar?" I demanded furiously.

Omar's face furrowed and his eyes widened slightly at the sight of the caller ID on the phone, but he said nothing. Filled with a sudden rage, I slammed my right fist into the side of his face and his head thumped against the side wall of the vehicle. The sound of it was like a gong going off and eventually, his head slumped forward briefly. With my right hand, I gripped him by his woolly hair and pulled his head back towards me. He was slightly dazed, but conscious.

"Answer the call," I said, handing him the phone, "But make sure that when you talk, you talk as if everything is normal. Do you understand me?"

"Yes, yes," he said with defeat in his voice. "Yes, I will do that."

"Answer it now, Omar," I growled.

Omar slid his trembling finger across the screen and answered the call.

"Hello," he said in plain English.

"Omar," said the voice of Younis. "I have been thinking and I have come to a decision."

I nodded at Omar to respond normally, as he normally would.

"Uh, yes," he replied.

"If it is decided by Suleiman that the hostages should be killed, then so be it. We can no longer afford for this charade to continue. It is time that we take the money and move on to the next project. I wanted to phone to let you know that I have come to this decision, so you know that, if he decides that the hostages ought to be eliminated, that is fine. Is that clear?"

"Uh, yes, yes," said Omar.

"What is wrong with you, man? You sound strange," said the voice of Younis through the loudspeaker. "Have you been drinking again?"

"Yes, I have had a few," said Omar in the blue light of the cell phone screen.

I nodded vigorously at Omar to continue the conversation with the man I had put my trust in for so long.

"I am fine, boss. I'll be fine in the morning and if Suleiman decides that is what is to be done, then so be it."

There was a brief pause, and I could only imagine what Younis was thinking through, perhaps accepting that Omar was drunk again, after all, he had been known for doing this.

"Very well," said the voice of Younis. "I will await the decision of Suleiman on the official call from the Kaminski offices tomorrow. Goodnight, Omar."

"Goodnight, boss. Thank you. Goodnight," said Omar, gripping the phone.

I hung up and struggled to absorb this astonishing revelation. How could it be that someone right at the top of the organization, in the upper echelons of power in the Kaminski organization, had betrayed us all and was actively involved with the kidnappers?

It was so unbelievable; it was nothing short of jaw-dropping. My mind was spinning with a thousand thoughts at the realization of it all and I stared at the terrified face of Omar with renewed hatred and rage.

"So, he has been part of this all along," I growled. "Younis Bader."

Omar said nothing but just nodded weakly with his wide, bloodshot eyes.

"Well," I said, "this is certainly a surprising development, but we have things to do. We must get moving. Start the fucking truck, Omar. Do it now."

Thankfully, the ancient engine started on the third attempt. The heater plugs apparently had had time enough to heat the diesel in the compression chambers. The engine sounded extremely loud in the cab and instantly my fear was that we would have gained the attention of the revellers at the celebrations nearby. But there was nothing else for it - we had to move on. I instructed Omar to reverse into the darkness and turn right, keeping as far away from the settlement as possible as we circled around and headed towards where I knew Trevor and Darius to be hiding out in the dunes. Once we arrived at the familiar landmark of the derelict factory, I told Omar to stop the vehicle, apply the handbrake and climb out. Still pointing my weapon at him I told him to walk. All the while, my brain was spinning with the unbelievable fact that it was Younis who had been in on this whole kidnapping all along. It had been Younis who had betrayed his boss Marek, betrayed us, but more importantly, betrayed the two prisoners. It was as bizarre as it was almost unbelievable. It took no more than two minutes to find Trevor and Darius, who were exactly where I had left them. It came as a surprise to them to see me approaching in the moonlight with Omar, now my prisoner and not their persecutor, to torment them.

"Get up," I said quietly. "We have to leave now. We are going to head down to the harbour, where our friend Omar is going to help us find a boat. We have some fuel in the truck and the rest of the bandits are still celebrating. With any luck, we can load up the fuel and get going without raising any stir."

By that stage, Trevor was too weak to stand, so I told Omar to help Darius get him to his feet and move him to the pickup truck. Through the humid night, with only a soft breeze coming off the sea, we trudged back across the soft sand to the battered Toyota. Once there, we lowered the tailgate and placed the painfully thin body of Trevor into the load bay. I sat in the back with my gun trained on Omar and told him and Darius to get in the front of the cab to drive the final short stretch down to the harbour.

This was done as quietly as possible, although I felt horribly exposed in the moonlight. The harbour was only 200 metres from the encampment where the celebrations were still ongoing and any glint of chrome or any movement down by the harbour could grab the attention of the partygoers. Everything could quite easily go to hell very quickly. Thankfully, we arrived without incident, and I told Omar to park in front of a pile of disused oyster boxes to conceal the fact that the battered pickup was there. Once the engine was turned off, we all clambered out and I instructed Trevor Nichol to remain where he was. With the astonishing betrayal of Younis Bader still spinning around in my mind and the fact that we were woefully exposed in the moonlight, I instructed Trevor and Darius to remain near the pickup while Omar and I went to inspect the boat on which we would make our escape.

With my gun trained on Omar, we made our way towards the vessels moored upon the hard sand, tied to giant steel pegs some 30 feet inland.

"Don't you even think of trying to mess me around here, Omar," I commanded. "Show me the boat—the fastest one, which runs on petrol, one which is reliable. Do you understand?"

"Yes, yes," he replied. "I know exactly which boat to use."

Eventually, we arrived at a long, thin wooden vessel. Compared to the others that lay there in the shallow waters, it appeared to be newer. Immediately, I nudged Omar with the muzzle of the rifle in his back, instructing him to move towards the stern of the boat, where the engine was mounted on the transom. A quick inspection revealed it to be a Mercury 100cc motor, which had been raised to protect the propeller from the sand. Sure enough, it appeared to be new and serviceable compared to the others I could see in the moonlight, and it was also true that the boat held no petrol at all. Omar had not been lying when he said that Suleiman had guarded the fuel.

"Right," I said to Omar, "this will do. Let's go back and get the petrol and have it loaded here."

Wasting no time, we made our way back across the sand to the vehicle where Trevor and Darius were. Trevor Nichol was still lying in the load bed, and I told Darius to help him out, making him comfortable on the sand next to the vehicle while we moved the fuel. Once done, I instructed Omar to begin carrying loads of containers of petrol to the waiting boat. He started doing this and Darius immediately began helping. The transfer of the fuel from the pickup to the boat took less than 5 minutes and eventually, it was time for us to move Trevor onto the waiting vessel.

The three of us returned to the truck and I crouched down before whispering to Trevor,

"It's time to get out of here. We're going to take you and put you in a boat. All going well, we'll be leaving here in the next 15 minutes and we're going to make our way out to the Kaminski vessel. Is that clear?"

"That's fine," he said weakly. "Thank God."

I stood up and instructed Omar and Darius to lift Trevor from under his arms. But in my mind, the weight of responsibility was now greater than ever. That, plus the astonishing revelation that I had just heard and had not spoken of—Younis Bader, the number two man at the helm of power in the Kaminski Logistics organization, had been in on the kidnapping all along. I still could not get my head around that fact. It was jaw-dropping to me, but I chose to remain quiet and say nothing. Omar would have his day in a Kenyan court, and I knew full well that leniency was not something they offered when it came to kidnappers and pirates. No, Omar would be spending the rest of his life in a Kenyan jail cell, of that there was no doubt.

A couple of minutes later, the four of us arrived at the boat. I instructed Omar and Darius to help Trevor in and make him comfortable on the wooden floorboards. Next, I called Darius and Omar, and we made our way up the mooring rope to the giant steel peg that was jammed into a concrete slab.

"Untie it now, make it fast," I told Omar.

Omar busied himself while Darius hunched down in the moonlight, acutely aware that we were exposed, while all along the music and celebrations continued only 200 metres from where we crouched. Thankfully, we managed to untie the heavy rope without any problem, and I hissed at Omar to coil it up as we made our way back to the boat. Once there, I made my way around to the stern and readied the motor by inserting a fuel pipe into one of the opened 20-litre containers of fuel. I squeezed the bladder on the fuel system to make sure the engine was primed and then checked to see if the ignition system was ready to go. With any luck, we would be able to push out silently into the quiet waters of the harbour, start the engine and be gone before anyone noticed.

Finally, I instructed Omar to walk ahead of me as I returned to the pickup one last time to collect the rocket launcher and the three rockets we had removed from the armoury.

This was an insurance clause I had decided on getting in case of any untoward situations during our escape. Omar carried the launcher and one of the rockets, while I took the others, all the while keeping the AK-47 trained on his back. We arrived at the boat, and I told Omar to jump in, something I believe came as a bit of a surprise to him. He did so without question. Then, Darius and I began pushing the boat out. At first, it felt like it would not budge, but eventually, with a bit of renewed effort, I heard the sand scraping under the wooden hull as it became free and began shifting back into the placid grey waters of the harbour. It was when the water was waist deep that I hopped into the vessel and stood to remove the tunic that I had donned at Omar's shack. I noticed that Trevor Nichol had picked himself up and taken a seated position against the side of the wooden hull, his eyes suddenly alive and sparkling in the moonlight at the prospect of our escape. A half-smile formed on my face as I saw the hope in his eyes. But it was then that all hell broke loose.

Suddenly, from up the beach near the settlement, there was the sound of manic screaming. At first, I thought there was some kind of disagreement at the celebration, but it soon became apparent that someone had seen us moving about in the harbour in the moonlight and the alarm was being raised.

Almost immediately, there were sounds of random popping gunfire in the night, and for the first time all evening, the music—the repetitive, terrible pounding music—stopped suddenly and was replaced by the angry screaming of a mob of drunken men. Knowing that now it was more urgent than ever that we get started, I scrambled to the back of the long, thin boat and began yanking the pull start of the Mercury engine in an effort to get it going, but the engine simply turned over and made a "putt-putt-putt" sound. There was nothing. Frantically, I squeezed at the bladder on the fuel system, desperately forcing petrol into the system, and then quickly pulled once again at the spring-loaded mechanism, but again, nothing, and the sound of the men coming down the slope towards the harbour was louder than ever. My heart sank as I turned to look and in the moonlight, I saw them moving as a solid mass of humanity, their weapons glinting in the moonlight. Suddenly, there were spurts of water all around, and sounds of bullets slamming into the wooden hull of the boat. We were under attack by a horde of drunken bandits and now escape had become almost impossible.

Wasting no time, I handed my gun, the AK-47, down to the seated figure of Trevor Nichol.

"Keep this pointed at Omar," I said hurriedly.

"It'll be my pleasure," said Trevor Nichol, his voice now strong.

"Darius," I said, "you keep priming the engine and pulling the pull start. Do you hear me?"

"Yes, yes, I'll do that, Jason," he replied.

All the while Omar sat huddled against the side of the hull of the boat, trembling and whimpering in fear. Quickly, I lifted the RPG launcher and wasted no time screwing one of the rockets into the end. After a quick check of its functions and flicking a few switches, I stood up in the hull, which was rocking wildly with Trevor's frantic attempts to start the engine. With the bullets flying all around me, I aimed the rocket launcher at the mob making their way down the beach and pulled the trigger. The immediate sound was hollow, like a tube being hit with a plank, followed by a roaring, whooshing sound that I had heard only that afternoon when young Alex had been killed by the same weapon. The rocket left a trail of sparks as it flew, and it connected with the horde of men and exploded in a violent ball of fire. Bodies were ripped apart, and limbs and torsos were blasted into the air as the night was lit up by the flames of death.

"Good shot!" shouted Darius as the engine fired up.

But there was one more thing I wanted to do. Knowing that most of the men who would want us dead were themselves now dead, I reached down into the filthy hull of the boat and grabbed a second rocket, screwed it into the end of the launcher, and as the boat drifted further away, the house of Suleiman Abdi—the house that contained the $3,000,000—came into view. Standing on the swaying floorboards of the boat, I lifted the rocket, looked through the sights and pulled the trigger. Once again, as before, the rocket left the launcher with a hollow bang and then flew true and straight, leaving a trail of fire. I screwed the final rocket onto the end of the launcher, stood up once again, took aim at the armoury and squeezed the trigger. What followed was an even greater explosion and we felt the compression of the blast when it hit us on the water as the fuel and ammunition went up in a massive explosion.

Without wasting time, I placed the rocket launcher on the deck of the boat and hurried back towards the transom where Darius stood, by the now-purring engine. However, as I picked my way aft, a grim discovery stopped me in my tracks. Amid the chaos, I had been oblivious to the fate of Omar—I had no idea. He had taken a bullet, one that had gruesomely removed the top left section of his head. The dead man's eyes, still wide with horror and a stream of chunky brain matter and blood had run down the side of his face, staining the cream-coloured shoulder of his dishdasha. Omar was dead, a victim of his own comrades. One of the bullets, intended to stop our escape, had claimed his life instead. *Well, there's nothing you can do now, Green. But considering what you know, it's best to keep quiet for now.*

It was somewhat disappointing, knowing that Omar would not face the justice he deserved. The thought that he would not spend his life in a Kenyan jail angered me. His exit had been quick and painless, unlike the suffering he had inflicted on the other men in the boat. Nonetheless, there was no time for such thoughts, I knew we had to get moving.

With the motor now running, I made my way to the stern, took control of the tiller and revved the engine. Almost immediately, the craft veered off to the left towards the shoreline, then headed out into the open water, eastward, away from the coast of Somalia. In my mind, I knew that escaping the kidnappers was just the beginning. Ahead lay great danger and finding the Kaminski vessel would be akin to finding a needle in a haystack without navigation equipment. Looking up towards the moon and stars for guidance, the lights and fires of the burning compound grew more and more distant behind us. Keeping a slow pace and doing my best to navigate, we headed east over the matt grey waters of the ocean at night. We had enough fuel but added to the dangers we currently faced, there was the problem of how we would approach the Kaminski vessel. To all intents and purposes, we would appear to be an unwelcome guest, the type normally associated with piracy. Approaching the Kaminski vessel with only physical waving or signalling as a means of contact seemed futile. Then, I remembered the two cell phones in my pocket—one belonging to Omar and the other to the guard Faizal I had dispatched when we left the prison cell. So, with the steady putt-putt of the engine in the background, we made our way over the dark featureless waters into the black chasm and the unknown ahead.

Some 15 minutes later, I made my way back to Omar's lifeless body, slumped near the centre of the boat. Under the moonlight, his vacant eyes stared back at me, prompting a decisive moment. I no longer wished to share space with him, dead or alive. I could still smell his body odour. With a firm grip on the top of his dishdasha and the belt at his waist, I hoisted his body and flung it over the rough wooden side of the boat into the dark waters below. As his form disappeared into the sea, I turned to face Darius and Trevor. In the moonlight, their eyes met mine and Darius gave a short nod of approval. He, too, desired no more of Omar's presence. With the body gone, my focus shifted to our dire situation. Stranded 20 kilometres off the coast of Somalia in an unfamiliar vessel, our goal was to reach the Kaminski ship, located roughly 100 kilometres away. The task seemed nearly impossible, and my only hope lay in the two cell phones acquired during our escape. Opting not to use Omar's phone, which held crucial evidence, I selected the guard's phone instead. Seating myself, I pondered our next move. Glancing at the screen, I noticed a weak signal, evidence that Somalia's basic cell phone infrastructure could reach us even 20 kilometres out to sea. I knew further travel would sever our fragile link to communication. Yet, contacting the Kaminski ship remained a daunting challenge. Stripped of all my radio and communications equipment during the failed hostage rescue, I was clueless about the ship's number or even the contact details for Kaminski's offices in Poland.

"Time to be resourceful, Green," I muttered to myself.

Then, it hit me. There was one number etched in my memory, one I could never forget. Colonel Callum Jackson. *It's worth a shot, Green. Just pray he answers.*

With the phone's battery perilously low, displaying only one bar, I understood the gravity of our situation. I had perhaps three or four attempts before we were left in silence. Taking a deep breath, I dialled the number. The first attempt was met with silence, then a garbled message I assumed was Somali. The connection failed.

Glancing at Trevor and Darius, I saw a mixture of hope and fear in their eyes. It all rested on me. I dialled again, focusing on the screen's single battery bar. To my immense relief, I soon heard a familiar clicking and then ringing. Struggling to contain my relief, I listened intently.

"Yes, who is this?" a gruff voice answered, irritation evident.

"Colonel Jackson, it's Green. We have an emergency," I blurted out, the wave of relief becoming overwhelming as I recognized his voice.

I quickly briefed him on our situation, the hostages' extraction, our location approximately 20 kilometres offshore, heading east with limited fuel, no water, food, or medication and our desperate attempt to locate the Kaminski vessel without navigation tools.

"Green, you made it out?" the Colonel sounded surprised.

"I did," I replied, "but it wasn't easy."

"I'll contact the Kaminski ship immediately and tell them to look for you. Well done for making it out, we had almost lost hope."

"Thanks," I said, aware that every second mattered. "We'll continue east but won't venture more than 80 kilometres offshore. Please, urge them to send a search party now."

"Roger that, Green. We'll find you," he assured, just as the phone's battery died.

Now truly alone in the middle of the ocean, I couldn't let my deep fears show to the rescued hostages. I mustered cheerfulness and optimism as I moved back to the transom and the motor.

"Looks like they'll be sending a search party. We might make it out of here by morning," I announced.

The idling motor responded to the throttle on the first try. Keeping the revs low and navigating by the stars, we ventured into the night, surrounded by the grey swell of the Indian Ocean. Two hours later, as dawn began to break, revealing a salmon-pink line on the horizon, I stopped the engine. Overcome with exhaustion, aches, and pains, I addressed Darius and Trevor, who were huddling against the frigid breeze.

"We're going to have to stop here, gentlemen. We have limited fuel, so this is where we'll stay for the time being."

Amid the overwhelming exhaustion and the lingering ache from the savage beating I had endured the previous day, a new discomfort emerged. An acute, gnawing thirst. My tongue had swollen within the confines of my mouth, and every pore on my body seemed to cry out for life-giving water. Yet, there we were, adrift in an endless expanse of sea, surrounded by miles of saltwater that mocked our desperation with its undrinkable vastness. This critical oversight in our escape plan gnawed at me. Although our preparations had been hurried, with fuel as the primary concern, I now wished I had spared a thought for water, especially since I had Omar to assist with the labour at the time.

As the pale morning light ushered in the humidity, it was clear the day would be unforgivingly hot. Our vessel, rickety and bare, offered no respite from the relentless sun. My gaze shifted to Trevor Nichol, who lay huddled on the deck of the boat. If he had seemed unwell the day before, he now looked to be on death's doorstep. A shiver of fear coursed through me at the thought of losing him to the harsh elements. Darius, beside him, did what he could to provide comfort, though he too appeared increasingly frail and weakened by our ordeal. I chose to keep my mounting fears to myself, acutely aware of the ever-present danger of hostile forces, armed men who might emerge at any moment, intent on ending our lives. In an effort to stay vigilant, I fought the urge to close my eyes, clinging instead to a sliver of desperate hope. I hoped against hope that

Colonel Jackson had managed to contact the Kaminski ship, and that a search operation was already underway. The very thought offered a faint glimmer of solace in our grim situation, a thread to hold on to in the vast, indifferent expanse of the ocean.

Hour after hour, we sat in agonizing silence as the sun rose, its ferocious glare baking us alive. The reflection of the endless heaving expanse of water around us only intensified the heat. It felt as though life itself had abandoned us, leaving us isolated in the middle of nowhere, with no land in sight and no means of discerning our location. My fears grew that we were drifting further from any point of rescue by the crew of the Kaminski vessel. Sometime around midday, when the sun's fury was at its peak, exhaustion and delirium began to take hold. In desperation, I splashed my face with seawater, trying futilely to ward off the sleep that threatened to engulf me. It was then, amidst my struggle to remain conscious, that I heard it. Initially, I thought it was a dream or hallucination—a sound so out of place in the silent expanse that I doubted its reality. But the sound grew louder: the steady thrum of a helicopter.

Squinting against the glaring sun, I frantically scanned the sky, praying it wasn't a figment of my imagination. Eventually, I spotted it: a dark pinprick near the sun. The speck in the vast blue sky grew larger and the sound louder, confirming it wasn't a hallucination. It was the chopper that had carried us from Kenya to the Kaminski vessel. The message had gone through. Colonel Jackson had managed to contact the ship to send out a search party. In a desperate bid to signal the helicopter, I rummaged through the boat, lamenting the lack of reflective objects. Ultimately, I found a battered aluminium bailing bucket. Holding its bottom side up to the sun, I attempted to catch the pilot's attention with its base. Thankfully, the pilots were conducting their search in a meticulous grid pattern, edging ever closer.

My heart raced with the fear that they might move on to another area and miss us completely.

But, by some miracle, they didn't. Roughly 15 minutes later, my frantic attempts at signalling seemed to catch someone's eye on board the chopper. It immediately veered towards us, dropping its nose and approaching at speed. A wave of overwhelming relief washed over me; we were going to be saved.

"They found us!" I shouted, turning to Darius, who blinked back in disbelief. "We're going to get out of here."

Darius nodded, his calm demeanour returning as he turned his attention back to Trevor, who lay unconscious at the bottom of the boat.

The noise from the approaching helicopter grew into a deafening roar, the rotor wash whipping up debris and dust from the boat's floor and stinging my eyes. I waved frantically at the men on board, noticing the pilot giving hand signals to confirm they had logged our location and radioed for a rescue boat. Within less than an hour, guided by the GPS coordinates, the sound of two outboard motors heralded our rescue. Two RIB boats, identical to the one lost to the Somali bandits the day before, emerged, racing across the swells towards us. The rescue happened swiftly; the crews helped Darius and Trevor into one of the RIBs. Abandoning the rickety wooden boat, I threw the RPG launcher into the sea and climbed into the second RIB. As the engines revved, we sped off towards salvation, leaving behind the perilous coast and ocean that had been our prison. Relief, exhaustion, and a strange sense of incredulity mingled within me as we moved closer to safety, to life beyond the endless swells.

56

Chapter Fifty-Six, Krakow, Poland, Two Weeks Later.

The giant chamber of the St. Kinga Chapel, deep underground in the famous Wieliczka Salt Mine, was warmly lit by its standard lighting of five massive chandeliers along with the glow of ten thousand candles. At 101 metres below the surface, the grand gothic cathedral had been hand-carved from the rock salt over centuries and had only ceased to be a working mine in 1996 when the enormous underground labyrinth was transformed into a tourist attraction and a World Heritage site. Travellers and tourists, having been disturbed by the horrors of the nearby Auschwitz and Birkenau Nazi death camps, found solace in the astounding beauty of the carvings, statues and underground lakes of the salt mines. Naturally, the giant underground cathedral had long been identified as the perfect venue for classical music recitals, and this evening featured the Krakow Philharmonic Orchestra's dramatic renditions of Tchaikovsky's 1812 Overture and Wagner's Ride of the Valkyries.

Access to the chapel from the surface was down a giant criss-cross wooden stairway, with a lift provided for those unable to make the descent on foot. Running 15 minutes late was frustrating, but this was soon forgotten when I finally reached the roof of the massive subterranean cathedral and witnessed its astonishing beauty for the first time. With walls, floors, ceilings and chandeliers carved from pure rock salt, the glow of the lights and candles below gave the massive space an eerily beautiful ambience. The powerful music from the orchestra, positioned in front of the 300-strong crowd of Polish and international dignitaries, lent the scene an air of opulent grandeur and breathtaking beauty.

I wiped the sweat from my brow with the sleeve of the hired tuxedo I had picked up in London that morning. A steward handed me a crystal flute of champagne as I mused over my day. After my afternoon flight from Heathrow to Krakow was delayed, I had taken a taxi to the mine entrance and rushed down the wide wooden stairway that led to the chapel, just in time to witness the concert in full swing. I had arrived in Krakow as a guest of Kaminski Logistica. The evening's classical recital was part of a planned celebration of the two pilots' escape from their Somali kidnappers.

It had taken only an hour to reach the Kaminski ship once we were picked up by the rescue team. Both Trevor and Darius had been placed under the care of Doctor Mackiewicz upon arrival. It took 48 hours for the doctor to stabilize them and give the go-ahead for their transfer from the ship. The Augusta Westland helicopter had flown back over the Somali coast near where the hostages had been freed. Unlike the former hostages, I had chosen to look out of the window, and it came as no surprise to see the burnt-out buildings and remnants of the brutal firefight that had taken place there. Once again, there had been a fuel stop in the outpost of Mandera in northeast Kenya before the subsequent flight back to the capital, Nairobi. The transfer of the hostages to the private jet had been immediate and I bade them farewell before catching a commercial flight back to London that evening.

I had said nothing of my astonishing discovery and the betrayal of Younis Bader to anyone, choosing instead to study the thousands of text messages and recorded conversations on Omar's phone. The fact that Omar had made it onto the boat with us before his death had been mentioned, but this was of no consequence to anyone with nothing to hide.

The story had unfolded exactly as it had happened in real-time, with only the knowledge of Omar's involvement with Younis kept as my secret. Both Trevor and Darius had witnessed Omar take a bullet to the brain and both had seen me toss his dead body into the ocean that fateful night off the coast of Somalia. This was now common knowledge. Battered and bruised but lucky to be alive, I had returned to my London flat to rest and tried to process the shocking revelation that Younis Bader had been actively involved in the kidnapping plot from the start.

The messages, dating back over two years, showed that Younis had been in contact with Omar much longer, the two men having met at university in the Netherlands years before in their late teens. The kidnapping plot had been brewing between the two of them since the decline of piracy off the coast of Puntland. Younis had quickly ascended the corporate ladder at Kaminski Logistica, a testament to his affability and work ethic. But deep down, there was clearly a deep and evil greed that Omar and Younis shared. After several days of studying the messages in chronological order, I finally understood how it had all come about. An opportunity had been identified by both men, leading Omar to contact the former pirate and warlord, Suleiman Abdi. A plan had been hatched for the kidnapping, with the spoils to be split three ways. However, the paranoia and madness of Suleiman ultimately caused the plan to go awry. What was supposed to be a lucrative and ongoing business arrangement had fallen apart, like so many other criminal enterprises.

With Omar's cell phone fully charged in my left pocket, I sipped the champagne and made my way down the final set of broad wooden stairs to the floor level of the magnificent subterranean cathedral. At floor level, I pulled the invitation card I had received from Marek Kaminski and handed it to a steward who smiled and pointed me towards my seat. I nodded at the young man and quietly made my way up the left-hand side of the seated concertgoers until I saw them. In a row, two seats back from the front were the men I had spent my time in Krakow with. Marek Kaminski sat next to his beautiful wife on the right, with Barry Matthews immediately to his left. There was a vacant seat for me and at the end of the row sat Younis Bader. All of them were unaware of my late arrival and were clearly caught up in the moment, the rich, magnificent sound of the orchestra filling the massive space with joyous and uplifting music.

The three men looked up and smiled warmly when I reached them. Younis Bader stood up briefly to allow me to squeeze into the row and take my seat. Marek Kaminski reached over and shook my hand vigorously with an iron grip and a wide, delighted smile on his face. Next, I shook hands with Barry Matthews, who sat on my immediate right. The big man looked a lot more relaxed than when I had last seen him, clearly relieved by the success of the hostage rescue despite the loss of young Alex. He looked ten years younger. Finally, I turned to face the chameleon of Krakow, Younis Bader himself. The man appeared pleased to see me, but I noticed beads of sweat on his forehead despite the cool, crisp air of the salt mine. He thrust his hand towards mine and I shook it as I had with Marek and Barry. But Younis's hand was cold and clammy in comparison to the others.

As I held his gaze, I dropped my smile and looked deep into his dark eyes, searching for any evidence or sign of guilt. There was none, until the last moment when I was certain I saw his façade slip. I held his hand for a second longer, tightening my grip while staring unsmiling into his eyes.

Finally, I let go and smiled again, sitting back and turning my attention to the orchestra. The sheer volume and power of a classical concert, especially sitting so near, was truly exhilarating. That and sitting next to the scum fuck who had orchestrated the whole nightmare in Somalia.

I took another sip of champagne and placed my glass in the holder on the back of the seat in front of me. A glance to my right showed both Barry and Marek enjoying the moment with smiles on their faces. A quick glance to my left at Younis painted a slightly different picture. More beads of sweat had formed on his forehead, although he was doing a good job of appearing normal.

With my eyes focused on the orchestra, I dug into my trouser pocket with my left hand and pulled out the cell phone that had belonged to Omar. With my peripheral vision, I could see that both Barry Mathews and Younis Bader had seen me do this. I held the phone in my left hand and allowed both men to continue watching the orchestra. It was some thirty seconds later when I swiped the screen on the phone with the thumb of my left hand and the screen illuminated to show a series of messages. The messages were part of a WhatsApp conversation that had taken place between Younis and Omar only six weeks previously. I had purposely chosen that particular set of messages to show Younis as I felt sure he would recognize them immediately. Slowly, I moved my left hand over to the left to enable Younis to see the screen and read the messages. I turned my head slightly to gauge his reaction but all I saw was a frown on his now sweaty face.

A further movement of my hand towards him prompted him to sit forward and study the screen. It was then that I saw the colour drain from his face completely at the recognition of his own words. He now resembled a ghost and was seemingly transfixed by the screen of the phone as I scrolled through the messages slowly with my thumb. A series of angry texts back and forth between the two men clear for him to read. The name, 'Younis Bader Poland' in bold clearly visible. With my head slightly turned to the left, I watched as Younis began to squirm in his seat, his panic rising uncontrollably. It was then that I saw him stiffen in his seat as he readied himself to run. Wasting no time, I calmly transferred the phone to my right hand and pulled my left arm back ready to restrain him. My instinct was correct because it was at that moment that Younis moved to stand up. But it was too late and I gripped him by the back of the collar of his tuxedo, preventing him from standing. I noticed Barry Mathews turn in his seat, curious as to what was going on, but I was beyond caring by then. I brought the phone closer to his face and pulled him towards me before I spoke into his ear menacingly.

"I know what you did..." I hissed and the man clearly heard me above the music. "It's over, Younis..."

But it was at that moment that the cornered man made his move, and it was unexpected. With his right hand, he jerked his glass of champagne upwards towards my face, and the liquid flew directly into my eyes, blinding me temporarily. At that moment he dropped the glass and slammed his forearm into my left elbow forcing me to lose my grip on his collar. In a split second, Younis Bader was gone, rushing up the back left of the crowd of concertgoers headed towards the massive wooden staircase at the rear of the cathedral. Hearing the commotion, both Barry and Marek leant forward to see what it was all about, but it was too late.

I had wiped my eyes with the sleeve of my tuxedo and was on my feet following him. The music was once again building to a crescendo as I made my way past the seated audience, some of whom looked up at me with bewilderment. By that stage, Younis Bader was running and making his way past the confused-looking stewards and up the first steps of the massive timber staircase at the rear of the chamber. I picked up my own pace once I passed the audience and watched as Younis bounded up the stairway like a spooked rabbit in the headlights of a car. He stopped briefly, his eyes wide with terror and his face as white as a sheet. Seeing me in hot pursuit, he wasted no time in turning and racing up the next set of wooden stairs. It was clear that the man had panicked and was now doing anything he possibly could to put as much space as possible between us. But by then my own rage was boiling over and nothing would stop me from catching him and giving him a thorough beating before whatever action would follow with the authorities. The shame of his grand betrayal would follow him for the rest of his life, of that I would make sure. Behind me, the orchestra played on, the violins shrilled as the music built up to a crescendo, the stupendous volume filling the giant subterranean cavern.

"Younis!" I shouted as I bounded up the first set of steps. "There's nowhere to run!"

The cornered rat stopped briefly up above me, and I saw the abject fear and panic in his eyes. But the fight or flee instinct had taken over and his was to flee. I watched as he pulled himself up the next set of stairs with his right arm, his opened jacket flying about him as he climbed. With my legs like coiled springs, I raced up behind him trying to close the gap between us, but he was surprisingly fast. Up and up the criss-cross wooden stairs he raced, his mind filled with the blind panic of the guilty as the music played on to the mostly oblivious audience below. But it was as he approached the roof of the subterranean cathedral when Younis Bader sought to turn right and make his way further into the labyrinth of underground tunnels, that his shiny dress shoes, shoes with very little grip underfoot, slipped on the polished floor of pure rock salt that had been smoothed by centuries of footfall. The slip caused him to tumble forwards uncontrollably towards the top banister of thick wood that was the head of the stairway that led down into the chapel. Younis Bader hit the heavy banister at speed with his midriff and without any semblance of control. His legs flew up in a wild cartwheel as his body was flung over the banister into the empty space beyond. Below him was a sheer drop of over 50 feet to the rear of the chamber and its smooth rock salt floor. But it was by some last-minute instinct of self-preservation that he reached out and managed to grip the side of the heavy wood banister, his body slamming into the outside of the massive wooden stairway. It was three seconds later that I reached the top of the stairs and for a moment I thought that he might have escaped as he was nowhere to be seen.

But it was then that I heard the scream. It was one of abject terror and it was coming from nearby. I looked back towards the staircase to see his hand gripping precariously onto the wood, the nails digging into it for dear life. Below me, the music grew and grew in volume and the kettle drums of the orchestra thundered in the echoing, cavernous space. I skidded to a stop on the thick wooden floorboards and rushed over to the hand which was beginning to slip. I reached the bannister a split second before Younis Bader lost his grip and I saw the stark terror in his face as I reached down and gripped him by the wrist. There was a flash of relief for a moment on his pale face as he thought he was saved. But it was not to be. Dangling 50 feet from the roof of the magnificent underground cathedral, the sweat on Younis Bader's wrists and hands had caused his skin to be moist, slippery and almost impossible to grip.

Sensing I was going to be unable to support his weight, I brought my left hand down and held him by the wrist with my two hands, his weight forcing my own chest against the sharp edge of the thick wooden banister with my fingers digging into his skin. But it was a battle that was lost. In the last seconds of his life, Younis Bader looked up at me and I saw the mixture of terror and resignation in his pale face at his own inevitable fate. It was then that I finally lost my grip. I gasped as I watched his body dropping, falling backwards while all the while he seemed to be looking up at me, his arms and legs flailing. The vast cavern was filled with a high-pitched scream that seemed to mingle with the shrilling of the strings of the orchestra. This was soon followed by a loud splatting sound as Younis Bader's body slammed into the polished floor of the cathedral fifty feet below me. Instantly, his skull was split, his organs ruptured, and the chameleon of Krakow lay dead. Dead on the polished floor of the ancient St Kinga's Chapel in the salt mines of Wieliczka, a pool of blood spreading quickly around his head. Panting uncontrollably, I stood there with my aching arms resting on the thick wooden banister as the orchestra suddenly stopped and the screaming and commotion began in the horrified crowds below.

The End

Dear Reader

I'm guessing if you are seeing this, it means you have finished this book.

If so, I really hope you enjoyed it!

If you have a minute, I would be grateful if you would take a minute to leave a review on Amazon & Goodreads. They REALLY help!

If you would like to continue with The Jason Green Series, you can find the other books here: https://geni.us/QCVsT24

Why not come and say hi on my Facebook page? I love hearing from readers. You can find it here: https://www.facebook.com/gordonwallisauthor

Thanks again and rest assured, Jason Green will return...

Cheers!

Gordon

Printed in Dunstable, United Kingdom